Books by Theodore Weesner

Winning the City
The True Detective
A German Affair
The Car Thief

Children's Hearts

Stories by

THEODORE WEESNER

SUMMIT BOOKS

New York   London   Toronto   Sydney   Tokyo   Singapore

SUMMIT BOOKS
SIMON & SCHUSTER BUILDING
ROCKEFELLER CENTER
1230 AVENUE OF THE AMERICAS
NEW YORK, NEW YORK 10020

SUMMIT BOOKS AND COLOPHON ARE TRADEMARKS
OF SIMON & SCHUSTER INC.

DESIGNED BY EVE METZ
MANUFACTURED IN THE UNITED STATES OF AMERICA

1   2   3   4   5   6   7   8   9   10

WEESNER, THEODORE.
CHILDREN'S HEARTS : STORIES / BY THEODORE WEESNER.
P.   CM.
I. TITLE.
PS3573.E36C48   1992
813'.54—DC20   91-47018
CIP

ISBN: 0-671-64242-1

"THE BODY POLITIC" AND "PLAYING FOR MONEY" FIRST APPEARED, RESPECTIVELY, IN
PLOUGHSHARES AND AMERICAN SHORT FICTION. "THE HEARING" AND "SMOKING
CIGARETTES" WERE STORIES BEFORE THEY EVOLVED INTO CHAPTERS OF A NOVEL. EACH
APPEARED, IN DIFFERENT FORM, IN THE NEW YORKER.

For my Mom, Hattie Shehorn,
Mother of my life

CONTENTS

Children's
Hearts

LOGJAM

They flare before the children on the drive into Portland. Carl, out of work for more than a year and a half, wanted to stay home and give his time to a paper for one of the classes he is taking at Southern Maine; Dawn, having become the breadwinner—taking a teaching job she did not want to take—pressed him to come along and help with medical and dental appointments she had made for herself and the two children. "Saturday isn't a school day—it's a family day," she said.

Snow threatens. Carl drives but continues to feel anxious, with himself and with the paper left unfinished on his basement workbench. Dawn could have planned for this, he tells himself. She shouldn't have called him away from what he was trying—however unsuccessfully—to do. He knows the word *disorganized* will set her off—it is the world's charge against her and one to which she always reacts—and he remarks, waiting at a light, "Most of the problems we have have to do with you being disorganized."

She lets a moment pass before she says, softly, "Carl, you should have written Freshman English papers fifteen years ago."

"I didn't," he says. "It's what I'm trying to do now."

"I have news for you," she says. "You have two infant children to support."

Hurt and anger move through him; he hears himself say, "They're not *infant* children." Not in front of the children, he thinks, even as he adds, "You agreed to the plan—which nobody ever said was going to be easy. So either do it—or don't do it. Bitching about it is driving me up the goddam wall!"

"The big plan," she says, and it is clear from her tone that she is up for the battle. "Carl, you have no idea what I think of the big plan. I hate my job—did you know that? I do—I hate it with a passion. My own children—they pay the price while I try to teach a room full of spoiled little brats who couldn't care less. I really can't tell you how much I hate that job."

"You tell me every day."

"You—going full-time is the problem! We knew it wouldn't work, and it hasn't. Don't tell me I'm disorganized! There's too much to do and I cannot do it all. That's all there is to it. You want to see disorganized—look in the mirror!"

"What do you think *I* do all day?" Carl says. "I take Owen to day care—when I'm not looking after him myself. I take Eva to school and pick her up. I do five classes—which is more than full-time—and I work jobs at least half time, if not more, to bring in some goddam money! I'm working my ass off is what I'm doing—studying my ass off so I can get a degree and get a decent job so we can have a decent life so you and your whole goddam family can maybe stop regretting for five minutes that you married me! It's a lot of fun, Dawn, believe me—it is a whole lot of fun."

"Going full-time is what is disorganized—it's about time you faced it."

"Going full-time *is* a mistake, okay—I know that. Do you have to keep telling me so? I paid the goddam tuition—which we couldn't afford and it's too late to get back. And I'm going to finish the goddam semester—which is only four weeks away, I don't care if it kills me."

"What you should take is a course in common courtesy and intelligent discourse."

"Well goddam—maybe I will! Where the hell is it taught? Do you teach it?"

"You don't have to swear all the time, not in front of the children," she says. "Things are bad enough as it is."

"What the hell does that mean? What's bad enough?"

"Everything, especially your language. *Do you have to swear all the time?*"

"My language isn't the point! Point is—you could be making this trip yourself, it's not that big a deal, and I could be getting some work done on my goddam fifteen- to twenty-page goddam personal essay term paper in goddam Freshman English. I didn't mean to lose my job, you know. It was the recession, if you remember, and you agreed, Dawn—in case you've forgotten—you agreed to a goddam long-term goddam plan to get us right with the goddam world—okay?"

It's awful. All of it is awful—and spinning away, down through Carl's chest. On a glimpse over his shoulder, he sees Eva staring to the side, as if to ignore the melee, and believes he sees Owen—small Owen, who is four and will turn five in two weeks—lying on the seat facing away. Eyes front again, Carl has to brake suddenly in a gathering line of cars—just as he wondered if Owen might be sucking his thumb in response to the flak filling the air. Slamming on the brakes takes the fight out of him.

"I cannot believe my husband is taking Freshman English," Dawn says almost gently as they sit there. "A little college student diddling around with diddly little freshman girls while his children suffer because their mother has to leave the house every day before seven A.M. and spend the entire day with a room full of other people's children. It's not what I wanted in life, Carl, I hope you know that."

"What—is this a threat?"

"Yes, it is a threat! *This is not what I wanted in life!* It's not where I came from and it's not what I worked for when I did happen to go to college myself at a normal age! Yes, it is a threat!"

Carl blinks at last, feels a blur of hurt as he drives along; Dawn, he knows from her voice, is in a similar state, looking ahead through a film over her eyes.

At last he manages to say, "Let's cool it for now."

There is no response, which is a response.

Around them is the overcast November air. Snow still threatens and silence fills the car as they roll along. In the mirror he sees Eva staring through the side window in silence, as before, and not seeing Owen on the seat, imagines him doing the same behind him. Motionless silence. A family day. Family fun.

Carl's heart winces as he realizes what his children have just heard. To think, he thinks, that it is worse even than Dawn knows. For what he has been unable to admit to her is that his mind has been jammed for an entire week now in the composition of the personal essay which has been determined to count a third of his grade. That the hours he has given to it in the basement, over Dawn's old typewriter set up on his work bench, have been wasted. That he is a week plus behind in the schedule set forth by the young woman who is his Freshman English teacher. That losing his job has not been a blessing in disguise at all, as he had tried to believe, but rather is proving to be a massive psychological assault which has been hammering him all this time, over a year and a half now, and which Dawn with her degree security and family security does not, perhaps cannot, understand. That being thirty-four years old and choking like this has him on the edge of seeming to dissolve into himself and that what has been on his mind lately is throwing it all in and looking for a job anywhere even if it means they would have to move to another state, or—a temptation he has nearly given in to several times—crying out to Dawn for help, crying out to her to somehow take over, crying out to her that however capable he always believed himself and presented himself to be, he is undone, has failed and is breaking down, is losing whatever sense he ever had of what to do next.

Carl becomes aware that Owen, standing on the center ridge in the backseat, is taking looks at him. Parked in a supermarket parking lot— Dawn and Eva left several minutes ago for the dentist's office across the street—Carl believes he glimpsed the beam of one of Owen's dark eyes between the seats. Too out of sorts to indulge him, Carl has returned to staring through the windshield, thinking how the Freshman English paper—unable to get it to go, neither can he get it to go away—has him in such a relentless vise.

Something else he has not confided to Dawn—part of the reason, he knows, the task has become so difficult—is the importance the paper has taken on for him, which began to happen several weeks ago when he met with the young professor-to-be and settled on his assignment. Failing in his one try at college sixteen years ago, his desire this time was to be outstanding—something he wrote about in a shorter paper—and the very subject, on the young woman's suggestion, was agreed upon as the topic of his term paper. "A personal essay. Fifteen to twenty pages. Your major work for the semester." For his life, he thought.

"You have perspective on this experience, and I believe you're capable of saying something significant," the young woman told him. Words of the kind were new to him—so different from those he knew from his days in the shop at Maine Design—and the words themselves, from the moment she spoke them, began singing a song of hope in his mind. He had perspective, was capable of saying something significant. A gate on a world he had believed closed to him had started to lift. A little. As in the old song, he had been blind and was beginning to see.

He tried not to adore the young woman more than he knew he could afford. To his added amazement—using a library for the first time, checking sources, carefully following all the steps—he learned that the topic was one about which experts had conducted studies and written essays, and this also thrilled and inspired him. It meant he was an expert himself in a way; he possessed experience of value—in a topic to be realized in nothing other than the mind. For having "a good mind," as the phrase was used in the shop, was something he had started admiring more than a decade earlier, back when he first began to grow weary of the tedious repetition of his work as cabinetmaker and laminator.

Do a "bang-up job," the young teacher also remarked to him, and she would help him try to get his composition published, in the school paper—the urban college was filled with older students—or in *The Maine Sunday Times*, maybe even in a professional journal. The possibility of having something he had written printed seized him and seemed at once to be the key opportunity of his life. Overnight he became infatuated with school, with studies, books, learning, discussions, and he began to fantasize the surprise it would be for Dawn and her parents to see his piece in *The Maine Sunday Times*, and regretted that his own mother and father were no longer alive to see the turn his life was taking.

All he had to do—next—in this blossoming of himself, was write a great personal essay, a perfect essay really, which, given his new energy and new desire, he assumed he was going to do, until he actually began trying to compose the opening paragraphs and for some reason nothing even close to perfect seemed willing to come forth. He tried harder, pressed for deeper concentration, which seemed only to make things go from bad to worse. Within two or three days the problem was too profound, too unmanly and stupendous to admit to Dawn, and he hadn't. For periods of five, ten minutes at a time, he sat with his face in his hands and could think clearly of nothing. All he seemed to know was that his mind was like a logjam up on the Kennebec and that more logs were jamming up every moment. His anxiety was such that at times he felt like he was going to explode.

He blanches now to think how he fantasized going to law school, fantasized himself a leader in the community, a respected citizen, living in a big house, even buying and sailing a sloop of the kind his father spent most of his life building for wealthy, intelligent customers. Blindsided at the pass by Freshman English. His in-laws, he imagines, would try not to smile.

"You mad?" a voice says close by.

"What?"

Silence.

There is Owen's eye, watching him from between the seats. Left eye or right, it's hard to tell. It has grown chilly in the car and Carl wonders all at once if Owen is trying to say that he is cold.

"I guess I am a little mad," he decides to say. "Yes, I guess I am."

"Me?" Owen says.

Carl needs a moment to see that Owen's question is serious. "No, I'm not mad at you. Not at all. I'm mad at myself. It'll pass. It's nothing."

"Eva?"

"No, I'm not mad at Eva. Didn't I say I was mad at myself?"

"Mommy?"

"Owen," he says. "I know it sounded like I was mad at Mommy. I was, in a way. But it's because I'm mad at myself. What I was doing was taking it out on her. I wasn't being real nice."

There is the deep dark eye, which keeps studying him. "Why?" comes softly from between the seats.

Carl looks down over the top. "What it is—," he says. "To tell you the truth, I thought I could do something. I still think I can. I *know* I can. But—since I started doing it, I've had some trouble. Everything has gotten harder to do—I haven't been able to do hardly anything at all. So—it's been awful, it's been scary. I'm all jammed up."

"Scary?"

"Yes—like Halloween," he adds. "Scary."

Silence.

"I don't mean to be short with you," Carl says, looking over the seat again. "It isn't your fault. I just haven't been in a very good mood lately. All week."

Silence.

After a moment, as if coming to his senses again, Carl looks to see if he can see Owen's eye between the seats. It isn't there. Looking over the top again, he sees his hair, sees that he is on the floor doing something between his blue sneakers.

"Owen, what're you doing?"

"I don't know."

"Sorry if I seemed to bark at you. I didn't mean to."

"What's my name?" Owen says, looking up.

"What's your name? What do you mean? Owen is your name. Owen Charles Nevins. The Charles is from my father."

Silence.

"Is that what you meant?"

"Why's Laurie Lars?"

"Her parents call her that. Lars. I don't know where it comes from. It's a nickname."

"Why?"

"Owen—I don't know. I guess—because they like her. Maybe it's how she first said her name when she was a baby, something like that. A nickname usually means you like someone."

Silence.

"It doesn't mean, if you don't have one," he says, "that you aren't liked. It's just a way—of saying you like someone. Usually."

"You like me, Daddy?"

He looks back down over the seat. "Yes," he says, and smiles at last. "Of course I like you. I like you a lot. I like you more—as they say— than anything in the world."

"You mad now?"

"No. And I wasn't mad at you. I was mad at myself. I wasn't mad at you."

"Why can't you—what you said you can't?"

"What I said I've been having a hard time doing?"

He nods.

"It's because—well I think it's because I've been—jammed up. I wanted everything to be perfect, and what happened is things are harder to make perfect than I thought. Everything jammed up on me and I've been having a hard time getting them unjammed."

"What's—jammed?"

"It's like—when logs come down a river. A couple of them turn sideways and get caught. Others get caught, and pretty soon they're all caught. That's a logjam. Logs keep piling up and none of them go anywhere. You're like a little shrink, aren't you? You get your father to talk out his problem—and he doesn't feel so bad."

"You don't feel bad?"

"I feel better."

Silence.

"You felt bad, didn't you, because I felt bad?" Carl says.

"What's a shrink?" Owen says.

Carl thinks, well, it does help to talk, if only to your four-and-a-half-year-old son. "Another nickname," he says. "For a doctor who helps people work out problems they have in their mind."

"Doctor Shrink—is her name?"

Him, her. He tries to explain and thinks there may be no end to the questions coming forth, thinks too that this may be what childhood is, a stream of questions until the stream runs dry, at whatever age, and one is a grown-up. What also comes to mind is an image of himself as a childlike adult as he remembers, relives, the call he made to his teacher on Thursday, one of the days when he looked after Owen at home and Owen was taking a nap. He felt he should not make such a call to the school, at the same time he felt so anxious about his paper that his breathing seemed to be giving way to gasps. Nor did she help much, even as she tried. "What has you in its grip," she said, "is an unspeakable two-word affliction that strikes persons who apply words to paper, and the second word is block. I wish I could tell you how to get it to break; I only know that it'll happen in time. Keep trying. Take a walk, and keep trying. Leave it alone for a day or two, and keep trying. That's the best advice I can give. Good luck."

Leave it alone for a day or two. That part of her advice only made him feel all the more constricted. How could he—

"I don't have a nickname?"

"Sometimes you do," Carl says, looking back over the seat. "Sometimes I call you 'Little Pea Shooter.' That's a nickname—a term of endearment from your father. You see—Little Pea Shooter?"

"What is that?" He puckers his face.

"Well, it's a straw—through which you can shoot beans. It means— it's like another nickname, Little Pistol—they both mean a person may be sort of feisty. What it really means is that the person using the nickname likes you. Like I said. Is that confusing?"

Silence.

"It's not confusing?" He glances over the seat and sees Owen looking up at him with both eyes. "Are you cold?" he says. "I am."

Maintaining the angle of his eyes, Owen seems to nod in agreement.

Carrying him on his arm through the pneumatic door, Carl positions him into a shopping cart. "You didn't seem too crazy about Pea Shooter—so we'll look for something else," he says. Starting the cart along, he adds, "Okay? It'll be a secret nickname. At least we can get warmed up and kill some time while we wait."

Owen's face is close to his own in the seating arrangement provided by the cart. "What name?" Owen says.

"That's what we're going to do—go name shopping. See, how about this? Ice Cube. Do you like that?"

Owen looks at him, disappointed, mystified, Carl cannot tell.

"A little chilly, I guess, especially when we're trying to warm up. No problem—we'll try something else."

Owen, he notices, keeps watching him. "Green Pepper," he says. "What do you think?"

Owen puckers his face.

"How about this: Red Cabbage? Kind of cute, isn't it? Or Scallion? Do you like that? Little Scallion. I like that, although it has been used a lot. It's a cliche, as my teacher would say—like a piece of gum that's already been chewed."

Owen looks as if he agrees, as if he thinks, too, this isn't bad—this curious search for something new.

"Here's one," Carl says; Owen swivels in his seat this time to see. "Now this—I have to tell you, is something my father called me. Carrot Top. I always felt good when he called me that. It meant he liked me. You know why he chose that nickname?"

Owen turns his head side to side, studying him again and trying to think of the reason.

"The color of my hair. Carrot Top is a nickname for people with red hair. I liked it a lot. My dad always smiled, you know, when he called me that. He'd hug me, give me a kiss on the cheek."

"Where's he?"

"My dad? Well, he died a few years ago. Before you were born. He—well, he was what is called a boatwright, built wooden boats, no metal, which have pretty much gone out of style. He taught me some cabinetmaking skills, which I'll teach you too one of these days, Little Pea Shooter."

Carl pushes on. He thinks of how he so automatically liked his father and wonders if Owen has a similar feeling for him. His Freshman English paper returns to mind too, as if to say there's no getting away from its angry jaws.

The day he quit school, he thinks, almost clearly. If he started there—? The day he quit—what about that? There was snow—a dark fall day not unlike this, he recalls, although it was a weekday, not a Saturday. He was living at home still, nineteen years old. He borrowed his father's pickup because of the snow, and arriving at the small city campus, unable to find a vacant space in the crowded student parking lot, circled around and by the time he drove from the lot had made his decision. Just like that—school was over for him. No parking spaces and it's all too much bother, he told his disappointed parents, although from the beginning of the semester, every day, he had felt that going to school was not only too much bother, but was in fact too easy.

What would the bright young woman who was his teacher say to this information, he wonders, even as he knows it's too late, too something, to call her again. He fears she would say, sharply, as he heard her say to another student, "Get something on paper and let me read it—don't *tell* me what you're going to do." He has no wish to disappoint this one person who seems to believe in him. The loss of her faith would be the end.

"Here's something," he says, steering Owen to the side again. "This is a real possibility. Bamboo Shoot. Do you like that? Hey, Bamboo Shoot, time to get up and go to school. What do you think?"

Owen watches, doesn't pucker and doesn't say.

"Dear Bamboo Shoot," Carl says. "Just writing to let you know how happy I was to receive your recent letter from the U.S. Senate and to wish you Godspeed in your forthcoming negotiations with Czechoslovakia." Owen watches but doesn't smile.

Carl turns a corner. "Okay—how about this? Ziploc Bag. Not bad, do you think? Best wishes from Zagreb, your cousin, Ziploc Bag."

The supermarket is old and in a part of town where it seems to be dying a steady death and only a handful of elderly customers arc pushing carts along the aisles. Owen, he sees, continues to look mainly at him, waiting for whatever might come up next.

"There! Early Pea. Little Early Pea. Okay," Carl adds when there is no response. "Sounds like someone in need of a potty."

Owen smiles and Carl is amused and pleased that his little joke was not missed, and thinks, well, bathroom humor, it always works.

"You're going to spoil me—if you laugh at my corny jokes," he says close to Owen's ear. "Most people just *groan* at a joke like that. *Ooooh— groan*—bathroom joke."

Owen smiles at this too, and Carl sees that he is, in fact, having a good time—although on the thought alone the constricting vise gives him a certain squeeze, as if to remind him that he remains within its grip.

"Now here's someone we can ask for help," he says. "At last. The esteemed research scientist, Nobel Prize winner from MIT—Professor Meta Mucil!"

His smiling gets Owen to smile, and he cautions himself not to overdo it.

"His colleague, too," he adds, in spite of his caution to himself. "Professor Magnesium Oral Solution, vizz whom he shares da Nobel in chemistry."

Owen keeps watching, reassures him with his ready eyes. "Okay," Carl says. "Mustn't get too carried away here. We're on a mission— right? To find a nickname. And *you* are going to make the decision."

Owen makes an expression, as if to say yes, he's having a good time, and pushing on, Carl says, "There's another possibility. I like this one. Buckwheat."

As before, Owen looks back but gives little sign. "Maybe that's worn out, too," Carl says. "Like Buckshot. Still they're names I've always liked. Buckshot. Buckwheat. Chewed gum from the bottom of the seat, right—like my teacher likes to say?"

Owen seems to nod in agreement and Carl kisses his forehead, feels a rush of affection for him. "You know, you're a great kid," he says, pushing on.

"Oh oh," Carl says in a frozen food aisle, pulling over and whispering close to Owen's ear. "I think we've happened upon a secret meeting of the heads of all the families. To the left, there. Tuna Lasagna. Chicago. Beside him, Turkey Tetrazzini. Providence. And—oh boy—I've seen that next guy on television. Fettuccine Bolognese. Detroit. And his bodyguard next to him. Famous hit man. From Brooklyn. Chicken Fricassee."

He leans in, adds in a whisper, trying to get Owen to smile with him. "See over there? Chicago Bears linebacker. Beef Stroganoff. See how close he is to the family members? If old Beef is on the take, there goes the Super Bowl for the Bears."

"What it is," Carl says all at once, surprised himself at his mind's turn. "What I was trying to explain before—I'm trying to write a paper for school about what it's like to have wasted a chance, and then have another chance—knowing you'll never have a third chance; in this game it's two strikes and you're out, not three—and how it doesn't mean anything at all, isn't worth doing at all, if you don't do it extremely well. It's okay the first time to sort of do it; the next time, though, the last time, doing it like that isn't doing it at all."

Owen, close there before him, is looking directly at him and seems, Carl thinks, to know that he is speaking seriously to him, that his father is, more or less, regarding him seriously. Carl smiles. "It keeps running through my mind," he says. "That's about as close, too, as I've been to getting it sorted out. An elusive butterfly. What do you think, partner?"

Owen smiles, doesn't say. Carl has the cart near the side of the aisle and, close over the handle, he gives Owen an affectionate hand brush over his hair. "See what happens when you become your father's shrink?" he says. "You get this stuff from the bottom of the river."

Owen's eyes stay on him and Carl cannot recall seeing him so attentive. "Do you know what I'm saying?" Carl says.

Owen nods, not firmly, but his eyes hold steady, as if to try for the affirmative.

"Thing to remember about your nickname," Carl says, returning to the task at hand. "It'll be a secret between us. You won't have to worry that some teacher will say good morning, Q-tip, please tell us the capital of Bulgaria."

Owen smiles—he knows teachers and Q-tips—and a thought comes up on his face. "Ask the teacher?"

Carl needs a second to see that Owen has returned to his father's problem, that he has thought of something—*he thinks and is a person,* Carl realizes—that his instinct is to try to do something for this man, his father, who has confessed to him his need for help.

"I did ask my teacher," Carl says. "She told me to keep trying. And I have, but it's only gotten worse. Thing is, I'm older than she is—six or eight years—and she's very smart, and nice—I like her a lot—only I'm the one who has more perspective on things, even if *she's* the one who taught me that I do. Anyway—I should be able to come up with a solution to my own problem. Does any of this make sense?"

Owen's eyes continue to be attentive as he gives an uncertain nod, and part of another, to say yes, and Carl feels a rush that has him kissing him again, cheek and hair this time, and holding Owen's head to his own. "Thank you," he says. "Thank you for being so helpful." Carl cannot resist kissing him yet again, this time a smack on the temple. "Got brain power in there," he says.

They still face the task at hand, however, and Carl tries Bagel Chip, Paprika, Rolaid, Listerine. Nothing seems to catch, although, going on, Aqua-Fresh gives Owen pause—a line crosses his brow—but so do Speed Stick, Tofu, and Kumquat confirm that the mechanism within the ball of silken hair is on the job.

"Anything?" Carl says. "Nothing?"

Owen shakes his head and Carl perceives that the small boy he is pushing around has, as if before his very eyes, grown more confident of himself. Just like that, he has regarded him as a person and he seems to have grown taller and older. Owen *is* a person, Carl sees, and all along he seemed to have assumed him to be something less.

Pleased, coming upon Tangerine mix, he sings the title of the old song—he knows it won't catch—and as they make the turn into the final aisle, feeling both happy and silly, and warm now, he pulls alongside a dairy case and says, "Vait vun minute here. I am sinking vee sphott der U-Boat Captain der. Large Curd. You see? Ya, he is writing a letter home to his sons, Yogurt und Schmall Curd. Und der, his first mate, Spaetzle, from Hamburg, and yes, der chief engineer just coming aboard after shore leave, Pickled Herring."

Owen smiles with him, but gives no other response.

Finally, turning toward the checkout lanes, Carl thinks, well, it's time to disengage Owen from the small burden he has imposed upon him. In a halfhearted effort, he tries Rock Salt and Potting Soil, and Owen smiles, aware, it seems, that they are only jokes. As Carl guides the cart through an unmanned lane, he says, "We're just having fun— you don't have to choose a nickname—nothing to feel pressed about. Like I'm pressed," he adds, trying to make a funny face.

Stopping the cart, he lifts Owen and returns him to a seat on his arm. Pushing the cart into place with his free hand, walking on, he says, "Know what I mean, Jellybean—just horsing around."

"Ask me," Owen says.

"Ask you?"

Owen's nod is both certain and giddy. They are passing through the pneumatic door, reentering the chilled air where—a pleasant surprise— snowflakes mark the air white and ashen gray.

"Did you really pick something?"

"Yes," Owen says close beside him.

"You did, didn't you? Can you tell me?"

Owen is hesitant. They are moving before the dull faces of parked cars as, shifting his face to Carl's ear, he says, "Secret?"

"You bet. Just between the two of us."

"Wait," Owen says.

Carl understands that Owen wants him to pause while he tells him. Stopping, Carl catches a glimpse of Owen's child's eyes and their bright dark depth receiving, seeing all. "Carrot Top," Owen says, just audibly; his breath has entered Carl's ear.

A current continues flowing through Carl as he resumes walking, as he holds Owen head to head. He says, nuzzles, into Owen's hair,

"Oh—what a choice—that's a great choice! You didn't forget, did you—gee, nothing could make me happier than to call you my own little Carrot Top."

The car is before them, thirty feet away, and even as Carl sees Dawn and Eva within, a current keeps seizing him, stirring about his chest and heart, and he doesn't turn to the car but signals with a finger, to say one more minute. He carries Owen on past the car, to let the storm within have its way, feeling that a first log may be about to break free. What it is, his mind—as if it is the superimposed mind of another—seems to be trying to get through to him, is some one small truth. That is the key, some one small truth. It may open the gates, loosen the vise, he seems to know, and he pauses, holding Owen, and closes his eyes to let it happen.

It breaks. Just like that, it breaks. One small truth.

Oh yes, he does have more perspective than his wonderful young teacher, he thinks, and he will be able to tell her, teach something to her. One small truth may be the key. One small truth. He is back in that parking lot fourteen years ago. The snow is fluttering down, and he is driving along slowly with headlights on in the early evening, looking for a space to park. He is making his decision to quit, and what he is seeing now, the small truth coming through to him is that it wasn't a decision to quit at all, because he had never made a decision to attend, that looking for a vacant space and finding none was what he had been looking for all along, upon which small realization he feels the jam of logs undoing and bobbing, moving into the open, as he squeezes Owen to his face in relief—as, taking in a breath, he turns to walk back to the car.

VOKE-TECH

Burger King is crowded and Kyle Hart has to join a confusion of lines. He said twelve-thirty and he wants to show up at just that time. Whopper with extra cheese, large fries, Pepsi. The Combo. Lunch in a sack should help—a small step in his scheme to help his nineteen-year-old son, Jesse, get his life on track.

"Here or to travel?" the teenage girl asks and Kyle—he likes to think he isn't losing touch—replies, "To travel."

Four blocks down the street he turns his Buick Le Sabre into the car lot where Jesse works. Kyle's oldest son is an MBA candidate at Carnegie Mellon; his daughter, in her first year at the Kennedy School, is, like her father, taken with public policy and hopes to enter government service in the nation's capital. Jesse, the youngest, likes extra cheese on his Whopper and assists in the repair of European cars.

Foreign Auto Emporium has used BMW's, Mercedes, Jaguars, Saabs lined up for sale in front. Kyle drives around to the rear where overhead doors reveal two active repair bays. Jesse sees him and smiles, calls as he releases the trigger on a power tool, "Hey Dad—be right there."

The time is as Kyle said and the sack of food on the passenger seat remains warm. He notices that Jesse's jeep, parked to the side, is topped with a new crash bar. The jeep was his own gift for Jesse's sixteenth birthday, and, true, it was delivered in the wake of the separation. When they talked on the phone, Jesse usually mentioned his new car items, but he had not mentioned the crash bar. Probably because it cost a month's pay, Kyle thinks. Unless—another sinking divorce thought— the mentioning of such small things between them was being left behind.

He watches as Jesse wipes his hands on a gray rag. Jesse always arouses an emotion of fondness in him. Just the thought of him, he realizes, and the emotion surfaces—is in him now, as he waits, in the form of a proud smile. Jesse, as friends like to remark, is the most thoughtful of his children.

Head angled to hear something being said by an older man in coveralls, Jesse glances his father's way. Jesse's teeth glint as white as white paper from his tanned, grease-marked face. Jesse's good looks always surprise Kyle, as they do now. All those dental visits at his mother's insistence. What a set of ivories he has, a smile and good looks of which he seems unaware.

Here he comes. The man in coveralls is laughing in parting. It's obvious that the man—he appears to be the senior mechanic in the staff of three or four—likes Jesse. It's always been like that; Jesse is a nice kid, is liked by all.

Wait. The man has something to add and Jesse pauses, cocks an ear. Watching, Kyle remarks to himself, well, that is his son, a would-be mechanic, a dropout, a good-looking kid liked by all, smiling in response to something being said by that older mechanic. Kyle feels a tinge of jealousy over the laughter as it is shared with the older man.

Opening the door, taking up the sack as he slides in, Jesse says, "Hey—Burger King!"

"If you ate on the way," Kyle says, "I figured we'd have more time."

"Dad thinks of everything," Jesse says. "You already ate?"

"Not really hungry," Kyle says. The bed and breakfast where he stays on trips to visit his youngest son and former wife serves slight breakfasts, but he is seldom hungry when he is here.

"Whopper with cheese—all right!" Jesse says, adds on his way to his first bite, "Long live the King!"

Kyle, pulling away, feels again the old pleasure of having Jesse at his side. The vocational-technical school was Jesse's suggestion for himself—when he failed to complete his first semester at college—and is something Kyle has been working on, for Jesse's sake, ever since. Jesse needed an extra year to finish high school, and he dropped out of the overpriced college in Massachusetts before Thanksgiving. On another visit Kyle stopped at the voke-tech school himself, to look it over and to pick up literature. He talked to Jesse at the time about what the school might mean to his work and future, to his pay, self-confidence, independence, but when he mentioned it again, long-distance, a week later, Jesse said no, he hadn't had a chance yet to drive over and pick up the application form. It was his own idea and a good idea, Kyle reminded him. Better to be moving, as opposed to standing still, he added.

Halfway along the fifteen-minute drive, Kyle says, "It'd be easy to zip over here for classes, don't you think?"

"It'd be a snap to zip over here," Jesse says.

Kyle drives along. "As a matter of fact I've always thought this was not just a good idea but a great idea," he says. He adds, at last, "I'll say this once, Jesse, and leave it alone. Doing this will be your decision. Whatever you do—if it's going to mean anything—it has to come from within you. Not from within me. I could pay the tuition, too. But it's not that much, and the crucial thing is that you do it, so it's yours.

"You complete this two-year program, even if it takes three years. And an apprenticeship with a dealer. You'd always have a way to earn a living, and it wouldn't have anything to do with going on to college, or not going to college. You could become an expert Mercedes mechanic, for example. As I understand it—a Mercedes dealer takes you as an apprentice, they send you to a school they have in Florida every year or so to keep you up-to-date on new technology.

"Key thing is to keep investing in yourself. Always. So you won't end up dependent on circumstances that are out of your control. With training, you'd have a position from which to work. You can always be your own person. Do you know what I'm saying?"

Jesse nods, finishing off the Whopper.

"I'm sure they're nice people where you work," Kyle says. "I'm sure they like you and you do a good job. Still, they could go belly up any day, for any reason. It happens. They might decide they *don't* like you. They could hire a new manager who'd give the job to his son-in-law. Where would you be then?"

"Lenny did fire this other assistant mechanic, just last week," Jesse says.

"Why'd he do that?"

"Oh, he came in late. Was supposed to clean up one night and didn't do it."

"What's he do now?"

"Just out of work, I guess. I know he washed dishes a few days at Copper Kettle."

"Well, I don't think you'd be a bad worker, but it's always possible to lose your job. With training, you're not at the mercy of those things. That's what I want you to get a handle on—to do things you have to start doing things. If you're going to get somewhere, you have to keep moving."

"Yes, Dad."

"Okay, I'm lecturing, I know. But I believe it has to be said. Not only that—listen to me now—not only that, but one of these days you're going to meet some girl who'll mean a lot to you. You may want to get married. Or you may just want her to respect you. It could be crucial to your happiness—hers, too—that you're going somewhere in life."

"Yes, Dad."

"Don't laugh. Listen, I knew that college you went to last fall was a mistake. It was expensive baby-sitting filled with screw-offs drinking beer all day. I'd have been disappointed if you *hadn't* pulled out of that place.

"This school isn't going to be like that. It's not going to be wasting time. These students pretty much pay their own way, and the courses are well organized. They have an actual purpose."

"They do have mini-car races," Jesse says. "That's what I heard. In the automotive program. They build miniature cars, in teams, and have a race at the end of the year."

"Sounds good. Would you like to do that?"

"I'd love to do that."

"Go for it then."

"Yes, Dad."

He keeps driving and in a moment remembers to say, "You can always read on your own, you know, and be an educated person. You don't have to go to college to be intelligent. And anytime you wanted, you could take regular college courses, even go full-time to get a degree. A person with a certificate from voke-tech *and* a college degree would be a truly remarkable person."

"Hmm," Jesse says.

"I saw your new crash bar," Kyle says in a moment.

"Well, it's for safety," Jesse says.

Kyle especially likes the feel of the large building now that Jesse is here with him. The lobby offers windows that face attractive fields to the rear and a neatly arranged reception counter offers racks of catalogs from which he selected items on his previous visit. The hopeful feeling calls up his own first visit to college when he was young and full of dreams, a sensation that still stirs within him on autumn days as a new semester is getting underway at some nearby college. Learning. Books and knowledge. Has that intoxicating appeal ever gotten through to Jesse?

The man who interviews them—he happens to be the Night Program Director—couldn't be better, Kyle thinks. The man does a quick take on things—a father trying to get his son going in life—and after a brief exchange, plays a trump card. "Let's take a stroll down the hall and I'll show you the shop while we talk," he says. "You, too, Dad. By the way, it isn't 'mechanic' we say anymore, it's 'auto technician.' "

Along the hall, the man adds, "You get under the hood of a car these days, you have to know your stuff. Electronics. The Buick alone has three computers in there. You get into a Mercedes, a BMW—those cars cost more than most houses in the world—you don't stick a screwdriver into something to see if it'll give off a spark. Just like that, you can destroy ten thousand dollars' worth of equipment."

The man unlocks a double door and throws on a bank of lights. The centerpiece, a red car, highlighted, could be a sculptor's work-in-progress. "Wow," Jesse utters. Kyle gazes in awe.

The man lets the shop speak for itself, and so it does. Cavernous as a gymnasium, the glistening red car at its center, its walls are lined with gauge-covered instruments that resemble stoves and refrigerators on wheels. Unlike any other garage anywhere, each tool, cable, connector is in its place, is oiled, coiled, freshly painted, and every glass panel is clean, filled with apparent power and accuracy.

"We can make a car in here from scratch," the man says.

"Wow—*two* dyna-machines!" Jesse says. "Most *dealers* don't even have one of those. They cost a hundred thousand apiece," he adds to his father.

They walk and look around. Kyle is thinking, well, it's an entire life projected here. And it's as good and as honorable as any. Better than most, he thinks.

"Our instructors are the best," the man is saying. "Nothing is assumed. Our students are taken through every step and phase and they have to know it all or they don't graduate. You can't be right four times out of five when you're repairing a car. Someone's life could be at stake."

He has walked them into an adjacent space where yet another vehicle is positioned on a rectangular bench in the room's center. "These cars are given to us by dealers," he says. "This Chevrolet came from a local dealer, was damaged in unloading. The dealers are desperate for first-class auto technicians. We have graduates in the state right now making fifty to sixty thousand a year."

A side room is lined with lockers and has two circular sinks in the center, operated by foot bars. "Students keep their tools here," the man says. "You do have to put out some money for tools. About a thousand dollars. But they'll be yours forever, so we encourage that you buy the best and learn to take good care of them."

Close to his son, Kyle says, "Something, isn't it?"

They return through the large rooms to the exit. A smile of satisfaction is on the man's face as he opens the door for them, and Kyle feels good too. A group of men, he thinks, charged with love, passing a torch.

"Now, son," the man says in the lobby. "Next step's up to you. You need to stop back to be interviewed by the Day Program Director, Mister Vinto. He's here most of the time, so you don't have to make an appointment. Our enrollments are not real high, so I'm sure we'd be glad to have you. Standards *are* high, though, so you'd have to meet the requirements, maybe even do some make-up work. Course work is demanding; I won't kid you about that. Myself, I think a lot of young people in these colleges, boys and girls alike, they'd be better taking our programs, for themselves and for the rest of the world, but that's not the way it is, I'm afraid. One thing you will get here, I absolutely guarantee, besides the skills you acquire: confidence in yourself. You make it through one of our programs, you'll know there's something in this world you can do extremely well. You'll always have a place."

In the car, returning, neither of them speaks for a time. However hopeful he feels, Kyle says to himself, let it be. If it takes, fine. Don't press. Let it be his.

In a moment, though, he says, "Jesse—I'll tell you something. You decide you want to do that program, it would be an honor for me—to buy your tools. That way you could say, years from now, I paid my tuition but my dad bought my tools and it was something he got a kick out of doing because he was my dad and he loved me."

"So far, so good," he tells his friend Wolf Regus over coffee that afternoon. "We're going out to dinner tonight, the three of us, and I'm taking Jesse back tomorrow to see the Director of the Day Program."

"How's Jesse feel about this school?" Wolf says.

"He's not saying much and I'm trying not to ask."

Kyle has stopped by his former university world and Wolf, a professor of economics, has taken a coffee break with him in the faculty lounge.

"I picked out a dealer in the Yellow Pages," he tells Wolf. "It was a crisis. Jesse was having problems, had to get out of that fake college he was going to—he called and said he'd rather go to voke-tech and work on cars than do what he was doing. I used the Yellow Pages and got through to a service manager, a Mercedes dealer in Alexandria—it's one of the European cars Jesse's always liked. What was amazing to me was how this guy understood everything and how helpful he was. Jerry, the service manager. I told him I had a nineteen-year-old son who was at sea in life, who loved cars and wanted to become a first-rate mechanic. Guy could have said he was busy. He didn't. It was like this was the priority repair job. He took his time and laid it all out. Vocational school to learn the basics was the right thing, he said. Apprenticeship with a dealer. Specialize in one product. GM. Volkswagen. He was so understanding, it was like a glimpse into some level of human nature I hadn't seen in some time, not in the mirror either, I'm afraid."

"What's in it for you?" Wolf says.

"If you mean am I working out of guilt, that's part of it. The thing that's always been the hardest—inside—is the feeling that I left him, too. Problem here, though, is not being selfish, being unpossessive—letting it be his move and not mine."

"Tell you something I've never told anyone, you no-good sonofabitch," Wolf says. "Of all the children of our friends. I like your other kids a lot, and I love my daughters. But of all the kids we saw grow up around here, Jesse has always been my favorite. He's a great kid. You know I gave him my old Ithaca twenty gauge last year. I hope you don't mind. I have so many shotguns I don't know what to do with them all. Well, that's not the truth. Truth is, I just like Jesse."

"Know what Jesse is?" Kyle says. "He's what is known as a good man. Do people still say that? That guy Jerry was a good man. The mechanic who tells you the truth about your car and doesn't try to screw you. The good master sergeant, the good cop. That's what Jesse really is—a good man."

"How could a father be any more proud of a son than that?" Wolf says.

"He can't," Kyle says.

"So what's the problem? Somebody did a good job of raising that kid."

"I don't want him dealt out—and I'm afraid that's what's happening."

"Remember the time Jesse saved that little Wiley kid's ass?" Wolf says.

Of course Kyle remembers, and he nods.

"Jesse's strength is what amazed me more than anything," Wolf says. "I don't know if I told you that at the time. I'm strong, and I know I'm strong, but I had no idea Jesse could call up that kind of physical strength. At that age. To be a good man is to be cool under fire—isn't that what we're saying here? Unpretentious.

"Anyway, besides his strength, Jesse's cool impressed me. I was coming up one side of Hagamore Hill and Jesse was coming up the other side. I first heard the sound—it was kind of a whine—I thought it was Jesse, because he was the only living thing in sight. Truth is, Jesse was more cool than I was. There was that Wiley kid and his goddamned dirt bike, hanging from the overpass. I still don't believe he got out there like he said he did. Handlebar's hooked onto a beam, and he's holding on with both hands—I still think somebody dumped him and his fancy bike over the side—and he's about three seconds from losing his grip and taking one hell of a free-fall to railroad tracks and chipped stones. Could have racked him up bad—coulda killed him.

"Jesse was so cool. I still can't believe it. He may have problems with math in school but he sure as hell calculated all the angles and forces of that equation in a hurry. Over the side he goes. He sticks his legs up and all he says is, 'Hold my ankles.' He handwalks headfirst onto the beam, reaches the kid's wrist, with me holding his ankles. I mean it was a *smart* thing to do.

"Holds the kid's wrist in one hand; with the other, from the elbow, he unhooks the bike handle, drops the sonofabitch out of the way. Props his other elbow, gets the kid's other wrist in hand even though the kid doesn't want to release his fingers from the wood. Says, 'Okay, Mister Regus.' *Mister* Regus—at a time like that! I'll never forget it. Then, as I bring him back by his ankles and belt, he *lifts* and *pulls* the kid onto the beam, and we hoist him over the railing. And there goes Jesse, heading around to the bank, and I say, 'Where you going?' and he says he's going to get the bike so it won't get hit by a train. Can you believe it?

"Tell you this, old friend. Jesse was fifteen when he did that, and maybe he didn't make it into University of Chicago or Harvard like other kids around here. And he may never do anything more spectacular than repair automobiles. But I'll tell you this: I knew he was a good man even then, and before then, and I've never seen anything to change my mind, and if I found myself in trouble, of any kind, and needed help, and the gods said, 'You can make one call, for one person, to fashion boat or raft or motorized flying machine, and the person will have to fight off alligators with one hand, shoot vultures out of the sky, dodge spears and read a compass, go three days without food or sleep and be strong enough of heart and mind to carry you back to the high ground,' I know who I'd ask for. Wouldn't hesitate. That's what it's all about, you no-good sonofabitch. Which I know you know. If you were a kid, wouldn't you want Jesse as your old man—auto technician or whatever? I sure as hell would. And so would you. I know you would. That's why you're my goddam friend and it's why Jesse is your kid and it's why both of us love him like we do."

*   *   *

Jesse is late coming home from work. They had agreed to leave for the restaurant at six and at six-twenty Kyle is having a drink he fixed standing in the painfully familiar kitchen. When Lucy comes downstairs, he says, "Thought Jesse got home by five-thirty."

"He works late one night—has to clean up or something."

"Which night?"

"I don't know; I think Tuesday."

"Today's Friday," Kyle says, thinking, well, nothing's changed. She doesn't even know which night Jesse works late. Nor is she ready to go. The same old rubs. He remarks, against his better judgment, "You really don't know which night he works late?"

She makes a face that says "Go to hell" and heads back upstairs.

It's different. On other occasions she would have fired a shot back, certainly from the hip, or made some remark about his girlfriend in D.C., he thinks. That she doesn't return fire is a relief to him, maybe, he thinks, a new phase in the ongoing hostilities.

He is outside, waiting near a basketball hoop he installed in that previous life when, in the handsome jeep, Jesse wheels into the driveway, stops, and smiles as both feet hit the asphalt. There are his white teeth in the midst of grease and dirt and tanned skin and he is explaining at once. "Couldn't get away even to make a call—had this neat old Jaguar that needed a flywheel and the guy who owned it was right there because he had to drive it to Boston . . ."

"No problem," Kyle says. "How's the jeep running?"

"It's great, I love it."

They circle the powerful box of a car as Jesse points to a single dent he hopes to repair when he gets a chance, and to the spare tire mounted on the back which, he says, is the only tire he has with enough tread to pass inspection. "I'm saving up to put eleven inchers on it," he says. "Off-the-road monsters—for the next inspection."

"Eleven inches wide?"

"Been doing off-the-road stuff, on weekends."

"What about on the road? Those tires cost in gas mileage."

"Not that bad."

"Who do you do off-the-road stuff with?"

"Oh, Andy Curwood mostly, Erskine, some others. Karen Cormier likes to go along."

Kyle nods, in awareness that what he is asking is less his business now than it used to be. Still he says, "Andy Curwood—I thought you two had a falling out."

"Long ago," Jesse says. "Old news. Still on for Chinese—I'm starving "

Mr. Vinto, the Day Program Director, appears to be a good man, too. Kyle surmises this at once, and feels added hope.

"We're not merely after people who have fooled around with a car in the driveway," Mr. Vinto says. "We're after people with brains. It's electronics now. Computers. Math. You have to be able to decipher theoretical relationships, not just take apart a fuel pump and put it back together. You have to understand not only the *how* but the *why*. Are you interested? Is that what you're here for?"

Kyle glances to Jesse, who sits in a chair to his right. He wants to answer for him, restrains himself from doing so.

"Yes," Jesse says.

"Okay—okay, good," Mr. Vinto says. "You'll have to get your application in, including your high school transcript. How much math in high school, how far did you go?"

"I did algebra," Jesse says. "Geometry and algebra."

"Two years of algebra?"

"Three," Jesse says.

"Three—you repeated?"

"One year."

"Well, math is important. We have people here who've been out of school fifteen, even twenty years. They have a difficult time, because they've forgotten so much. Should be easier for you, given your age and how recently you've been in school. Still, math is the first thing you should do."

"He's interested in starting on a part-time basis," Kyle says. "Maybe two courses the first semester. He'd like to start carefully and do a good job, before going full-time."

"Three courses is better, given the sequences that have to be followed and because some courses need to be taken in tandem with others. Electronics and Auto Shop, for example. They should both be taken the first semester. But he'd also have to take the math course. And it costs just as much to take three as it does to take two."

"Two wouldn't work?" Kyle says.

"I don't think so," the man says. "Not first semester."

"Jesse, what do you think?" Kyle says.

Jesse returns, it seems to Kyle, from a momentary journey. "What would the schedule be?" Jesse says. "I don't know how much time I can be away from my job."

Something is wrong, Kyle realizes.

Jesse is leaning in and Kyle leans in too, to look at the schedule the man is pointing at. There, four days out of five, every day but Friday, at eight A.M., is math. Is that what it is? Kyle wonders. Math?

"After math, see, Tuesday and Thursday," the man is saying. "Electronics Lab. Electronics Lecture is Monday, Wednesday, Friday, here, eleven to twelve. Auto Shop Lab, Tuesday and Thursday afternoons, one to four P.M. Even with three courses, it's demanding first semester."

Silence follows. Kyle doesn't look his way, but is hoping for Jesse to speak, to ask a question about eating lunch, parking, books, anything at all. He doesn't, and Kyle knows with certainty that something is wrong.

"In your court now," Mr. Vinto says at last. "There's an application in the catalog, tells you about having your high school transcript sent in. You don't want to include a transcript from that college you went to, that's up to you. Sooner you get your application in the better, though. It's only a few weeks away."

As before in the car, Kyle is afraid to speak. Then he says, "Well?"

"I don't know," Jesse says in a moment.

Kyle knew it was coming, still his heart collapses a little. "You've got to do something," he says.

"I've got a job."

"What if you lose your job?"

"I won't."

"What if you do?"

"I'll get another job."

They drive on. Kyle resists reminding Jesse that the voke-tech program was his idea, and he doesn't want to show anger or disappointment—the departed father come back to manage his youngest son's life—but nothing coming to mind is free of either helpless emotion. Nor can he look past an awareness that has been building in him since he arrived, that Jesse is divorcing him, keeping a distance from him.

He drives on.

"If you wanted to go full-time, I'd be happy to pay for it," Kyle says. "You don't have to work at all right now."

"I know," Jesse says.

They go along, reentering town, and drive along the street of gas stations to Foreign Auto Emporium. Kyle pulls in, and around to the rear. He debates turning off the motor, does so.

"Is it the math?" he says. "Does math—put you off?"

"I don't know," Jesse says. "I don't think so."

"You don't want to do it?" Kyle says.

"No."

Kyle looks at his son and doesn't know what to say.

They sit there.

"Don't worry about me, Dad," Jesse says. "I'll do something, sometime. Have to get back," he adds.

Kyle nods; Jesse leaves the car and returns toward the opened garage door where the older mechanic and a boy Jesse's age look up and smile as friends do.

Jesse is probably smiling in turn; Kyle cannot tell from his angle. The school application remains left behind in the passenger seat.

At the street, Kyle pulls up to look both ways. Only then do his eyes blink. They blink once, as they have at other times in his life. He'd like to go back, correct the mistakes he's made in his life, but knows he cannot. He'd like to give Jesse whatever room he needs, without losing him, but doesn't know how. He sits there. He has nowhere to go for the moment, wonders how he will pass the rest of the afternoon. He knows that he must enter the street to find out, and in a moment he does so, turns left, drives in that direction.

THE BODY
POLITIC

F ive-five and one-twelve, thirteen years old, out of an obscure
elementary school, a complete unknown, Glenn Whalen walks into the
boys' locker room to spin the dial of his combination lock. Emerson
Junior High. It's a school with a double gym with a whiskey-colored
floor upon which street shoes are never allowed.

The occasion: seventh grade basketball tryouts.

Glenn removes items from his gym bag and places them on the
bench. Two pair of white wool socks, white hi-top sneakers, gym shorts,
T-shirt, jock. All but the T-shirt are new. He has to remove staple and
paper label from a pair of socks, the jock from the box. The new
sneakers, a once-a-year event, promise speed, new squeak-grips on the
polished wooden floor, sudden turns, spring. This pair, he has told
himself, he'll keep strictly for indoor use, a promise he made to himself
in sixth grade too, only to break it during a sunny February thaw to the
more immediate promise of running outdoors with seeming lightning
speed.

The gym bag is new too—his first—navy blue with brown leather
handles, a spontaneous gift from his father as they shopped on Saturday. Except for the sneakers, P F Flyers, and the jock, a Bike—a slight
necessity, but his first and thus no slight event after all—the items are
free of racing stripes and product names, as apparently uncomplicated

as other forces at work in the era during which this otherwise unnoticed chapter in sports history is quietly unfolding.

Glenn and his father, Red Whalen—the two live together in an apartment on Buick Street, in the obscure elementary school district, just up the hill from Buick Plant Three where Red works the second shift—picked out the items at Hubbard's Hardware & Sporting Goods downtown. Glenn's list from school did not include a gym bag, and he imagined carrying everything in a paper bag, much as his father always had a bottle in a paper bag nearby, in glove box, trunk, under the driver's seat. But his father had already tipped one of those bags a few times by midday Saturday, the last a sizeable snort as they parked in the alley behind Hubbard's, and there were the gym bags on a shelf before them.

"How you going to carry all that gear?"

Glenn, looking in the same direction, did not say.

"Let's do it right," his father said. "Fight them to the end. On land, in the air, on the sea." There was that reddish glow in his cheeks, the film over his eyes, his Mona Lisa grin.

Blue is the wrong color, though, Glenn realizes when a string of five boys—tall, renowned Ray Peaks among them—enters the locker room, each carrying a kelly green gym bag. The school colors are green and white, Glenn knows, alas, in this moment, even as he knew it all along. Green and white, fight fight! "Shoot!" he says aloud.

"Belly high . . . without a rubber," one of the five boys sings out as they turn into a nearby aisle.

Glenn's plain white T-shirt also identifies him as an outsider. It's true that other white T-shirts are present in the gathering of twenty-five or thirty, but each is worn by a boy who handles a basketball with his elbows out, or one who cannot get his feet, in concert with his hands, to comprehend the concept of *steps*. Then two more boys wearing white T-shirts walk in, but the two—they have to be twins—are blubbery with jelly rolls around their middles, with near-breasts, and each wears knee guards, elbow guards, and wire cages over glasses. Otherwise most of the boys wear kelly green basketball jerseys, although no such item was included on the mimeographed list. One boy wears flowered bathing trunks that he had outgrown perhaps a year earlier.

Coach Bass walks into the gym carrying a new ball, blowing his whistle, shouting at them to return the balls to the ball bin, to *never* take a ball from that bin unless he says to! Appearing then, making a jogging entrance from the tunnel onto the glossy floor, are the boys of the green gym bags. The five, Glenn notices, wear uniform gray sweatshirts— over green sleeveless jerseys, it will turn out—above white gym shorts and, laced in a military staircase braid into their white sneakers, matching green shoelaces. They are the ones, everything about them seems to say, who know the score, who already have it made at Emerson Junior High.

Coach Bass, ball under his arm, tweets his whistle, tells them to sit down. He paces to and fro before them, shifts the new ball hand-to-hand as he talks. He introduces the Locker Room Man, "Slim," who stands at the tunnel entrance watching. The best players and hardest workers will make the traveling squad of ten, he tells them. That's the way it is. This isn't elementary school anymore and that is the black and blue reality of competitive sports. A list will be posted on the bulletin board outside his office after practice on Friday. BUT, he adds, raising a finger. That's not all. Any boy—any one of them who has the desire. Who is willing to do the work. Can continue to attend practices. AND, from among THOSE boys TWO alternates will be SELECTED to dress for each home game.

Glenn sits, watching and wondering. Two alternates for each home game. It means everyone has a chance. Sort of. But does the Coach mean the *same two,* or two *new* ones each time? There are so many students here in junior high—hundreds more than in the small brick elementary school he attended last year. Building and grounds cover acres. And any number of ninth grade boys actually have moustaches, are over six feet tall. And some of the girls—wow!

The Coach blows his whistle again. He snaps, "On your feet!" and they jump, almost as one, as if the process of selection is related to how quickly one can get upright. All but Ray Peaks, Glenn notices. Ray Peaks—his arms appear to reach his knees—pushes up from one hand and is the last to stand. Still, he is the first to receive a pass, as the Coach snaps the new ball to him and tells him to lead a line along the wall of folding doors.

Glenn follows into the line and performs as instructed. He joins rows of five, backpedals, sidesteps side-to-side, starts and stops. However anxious he feels, he does not have the problems of any number of boys who move left when they should move right, cross their feet when they should sidestep, stop when they should start. He dribbles in and around strategically placed folding chairs. He exchanges passes along a line of others and takes his place at the other end. He follows through one line to shoot a lay-up, and another to rebound and pass off. He begins to perspire, to breathe more deeply, to relax a little, and begins to observe the others in their turns as he waits in lines. And, like others, he glances to the Coach now and then, to see if he can see whatever it is the man is taking in.

Junior high basketball. For home games the panels will be folded away, bleachers will unfold from either side, and the space and glossy floor—the surface is no less than beautiful, precious, an expanse of fixed lacquer upon which to perform—will offer a dimension that is possibly magical. Ray Peaks, Glenn hears in one of the moving lines, could play with the senior team if he wanted.

Glenn tries harder, tries to concentrate. However new he is to organized drills and dashes, shouts and whistles, it is becoming increasingly apparent that he is far from the worst. For while the gang of five seems to know all of the moves, any number of others, here and there, now and again, continue to reveal various shortcomings. And—the most promising sign to Glenn—going in on a bounce pass down the middle, to go UP! and lay the ball over the front edge of the rim without crashing into the Coach where he is positioned just under the backboard, he hears at his back that phrase which shoots him through with sudden hope. "Nice shot there."

Friday waits before them as the week moves along, but Glenn goes about life and school in his usual ways. He has never *made* anything like a team before, and even as he entertains his degree of hope, he hardly takes on any of the anxieties of expectation. Good things come home when you don't stand at the door waiting, his father has told him, and Glenn gives little thought to what it will mean if he does or does not make the team. He will probably keep trying, he thinks, on the chance of dressing as an alternate.

He begins to eat lunch with Norman Van Slyke, who sits in front of him in homeroom. Glenn's father leaves him a dollar on the kitchen table every morning for lunch and on his own Glenn has fallen into a habit of walking three blocks from school to a small corner grocery he spotted sometime previously. Cold weather has yet to arrive and at the store—Sam Jobe's Market—he stands inside near a red pop case to eat, or he sits outside in the sun. Lunch is a packaged pie, usually pineapple but sometimes cherry, a Clark bar or two and, from a glass-bowl machine, five or six pennies' worth of Spanish peanuts to feed into his bottle of Hires Root Beer, salty beetles, as he thinks of them—perhaps Japanese beetles, which are popular at the time, although he has never seen one—that he pops to oblivion between his teeth as he drinks his root beer.

Norman Van Slyke's looks made Glenn smile the first time he saw him in homeroom. Sparse hairs sprout already from the short thin boy's upper lip, just under his adhesive-tape hinged glasses, and his extensive nose projects out in the midst of this confusion like an animal reaching its head from a hole in the ground. Norman's features twitch; the periscope that is his nose seems to look around at times, to glance up and down, and to the side.

Glenn calls him Rat Nose at once, and the name brings immediate snickers of pleasure from the other boy. In turn, Rat Nose identifies Glenn as Weasel, and they take on the names and wear them along the street as comfortably as old sweatshirts.

After-school practices continue. Each morning, coming out of Civics and turning right, headed for Geometry, Glenn discovers that he passes Ray Peaks going the other way. On Thursday morning, the lanky boy utters, "Say," in passing, and on Friday, when Glenn speaks first and says, "Hi," to the school's already-famous athlete, Ray Peaks winks in a natural and friendly way that reminds Glenn of his father's winks.

Glenn also hears or learns in the days passing that the boys of the kelly green gym bags all attended the elementary school attached to the very end of Emerson Junior High. So it is that they had used the glossy hardwood double gymnasium all those years, stopped by after school to see home games, and, as it also comes out, played together for two years as teammates in a Saturday morning league. In practices, when teams are identified, and when they scrimmage, the five boys, Ray Peaks ever the nucleus, move as one.

Glenn's basketball experience was different. His elementary school, near Buick plants Two and Three along a branch of the city river, had neither gymnasium nor coach. A basement classroom served as a gym, under the guidance of the gym teacher, Mrs. Roland. Painted blackish-brown, its high windows and ceiling light fixtures caged, the room offered a single netless rim fixed flush to the wall, eight or nine feet from the floor and perhaps eighteen inches from the ceiling. The clearance was enough for either lay-ups or line drives.

No matter, Glenn always thought, for in gym class they only played little kid games in circles anyway and only once, in sixth grade, was basketball ever given a try. Mrs. Roland, whistle around her neck, glasses on a separate lanyard, demonstrated—to introduce that one game—by hoisting the cumbersome ball from her side with both hands, kicking up one ankle as she tossed it at the basket, hitting the *bottom* of the rim. Then she selected teams—which selections for any real sport, indoors or out, were always maddening to Glenn, as she chose captains and teams by height rather than ability. And she officiated the year's single basketball game by calling one jump ball after another, the contest lasting three minutes or less, concluding on a score of 2 to 0.

Tall boys will always be given the breaks, Mrs. Roland seemed to say. And if your last name starts with W, your place in line will always be at the end.

Glenn did play outdoors. At least a year before Mrs. Roland's demonstration, as an eleven-year-old, he paused on a sidewalk beside a cement driveway at the side of a church along Buick Avenue, and discovered not Jesus but basketball. The church was First Nazarene and the boys playing under the outdoor hoop were high school age. Glenn stood and watched, and when a loose ball came his way, he shagged it and walked it back several steps to throw it to the boy walking toward him.

"Wanna play, come on," the boy said.

Glenn was too thrilled to be able to say. He did walk toward the action, though, nodding, although he had just a moment ago touched a basketball for the first time in his life. "You're on my side," the boy said. "Gives us three on a side."

Anxious, Glenn moved into the area as instructed. The boy who had invited him—who was pointing out the sides, treating him as some actual person he had never known himself to be—turned out to be the seventeen-year-old son of the church's minister. Glenn had never encountered a generous teenager before, and his wonder was such that he might have been a possible convert to nearly anything, but no such strings were attached. The seventeen-year-old boy was merely that rarest of individuals in Glenn's life, a teenager who wasn't mean.

The game—Twenty-one—progressed, and passes were sent Glenn's way as if he knew what to do. He did not. He passed the ball back each time, another time bounced it once and passed it back, and no one said anything critical, nor cast any critical glances, and the minister's son, who was already a memorable figure to Glenn, said at last, when Glenn single-dribbled again and return-passed the ball, "That's the way."

It would seem that Glenn was being indulged, but something in the way the game was managed made it no less real as a contest. The minister's son had Glenn put the ball in play each time it was his team's turn to do so, and in time he said to him, "Don't be afraid to take a shot," and when Glenn passed off instead, he said, "Go ahead, take a shot or you'll never learn." A chance came again, and even as it may not have been the best opportunity, Glenn pushed the ball two-handed toward the basket, only to see it fall short by two or three feet.

His teammates recovered the ball, passed and circled, and the boy said to him, "That's okay, good try, try it again." In time there came another opportunity, closer in, and this time the ball hit on the rim, hesitated, and, at last, dropped through, and the boy said only, "There you go, that's the way," as if it were just another basket among all that might pass through such a metal ring and not Glenn Whalen's very first. Glenn continued with the game, too, as if nothing out of the ordinary had happened. But by the time evening air was descending he had grown so happy a glow was in his eyes, and for the first time in his life he was falling in love with something.

He had to be told to go home. When the sky was so dark the ball could be spotted only directly overhead, a black moon against the night sky, and three of the other boys had drifted away, the minister's son finally said to him that he had better head on home, it was getting late. As Glenn started off, though, the boy called after him, said they played every night at that time, to stop by again, and if wanted to shoot by himself, the ball would be just inside that side door and he was welcome to use it just so he put it back when he was done.

Glenn shot baskets, hours on end, entering into any number of imaginary schemes and games, and that summer and fall alone, until snow and ice covered the driveway, he played away a hundred or more evenings with the older boys, game after game, unto darkness. The games were three-on-three, although there were evenings when enough boys showed up to make three or four teams, and to continue to play a threesome had to win or go to the end of the line. Glenn loved it; he learned most of the moves and absorbed them into his system as one does.

And so it is, on Friday after school when practice ends and he follows along with the others to the bulletin board between gym and locker room and reads the typed list there between shoulders, reads it from the top—*Raymond Peaks*—down, the tenth name on the list is *Glenn Whalen*.

He is invited to lunch. In school on Monday, outside his home-room, one of the boys of the green gym bags—Keith Klett, also a guard—appears at Glenn's side and doesn't ask him but tells him to meet them out front at lunchtime. His house is only two blocks away, the boy adds; it's where they go to eat.

Seeing Rat Nose later, Glenn mentions that he is going to eat lunch with the basketball team, and he experiences but the slightest twinge of betrayal. When he gathers with the others by the mailbox, though, there are only six of them who cross the street to walk along the residential sidestreet and Glenn realizes, for whatever reason, that he is being selected by the five as a sixth man. He is being taken in. And he is not so naive that he doesn't know the reason; basketball is at the heart of it and some one person or another, or the Coach, has to have noted, as the line goes, that he is good.

Four of the five—all but Keith Klett—carry home-packed lunches in paper bags, and Glenn is asked about the whereabouts of his own. "You can make a sandwich at my house," Keith Klett says. "No charge."

So Glenn does—nutty peanut butter on fluffy Wonder bread—in a large kitchen and large house which if not elegant are far more middle class than any house he has ever visited in a similar way. He is impressed by the space; there seem to be so many rooms, rooms of such size, a two-car garage outside, a sun porch, a den; then, up a carpeted turning stairway to a second floor, Keith Klett's bedroom is larger than the living room in the four-room walk-up apartment he and his father have called home for the last couple years.

No less noticeable to Glenn's eyes are the possessions, the furnishings and appliances, a boy's bedroom seemingly as filled with sports equipment as Hubbard's Hardware, and, on a counter, a globe which lights and an aquarium with bubbles but no fish—"the dumb jerk peed in the tank and they all croaked," Ray Peaks says—and model planes, ships, tanks, a desk with a lampshade shaped like a basketball and, in its own bookcase, an *Encyclopedia Britannica* set just like the one in the junior high reference room. And—the reason they can troop through the house at will, the reason to troop here for lunch in the first place—Keith Klett's parents are both at work.

Making a sandwich in the kitchen, following each of Keith Klett's steps, including the pouring of a glass of milk, Glenn follows into the den where the others sit around eating. Hardly anything has been said about basketball, and some joke seems to be in the air, but Glenn has yet to figure out what it is. Sandwich packed away in two or three bites, two-thirds of his glass of milk poured in after, Keith Klett, smiling, is soon on his feet, saying to Glenn, "There's something you have to see," slipping away to run upstairs as Ray Peaks calls after him, "Keith, leave that crap alone, it makes me sick."

There is no response.

"What's he doing?" Glenn asks.

"You'll see—it'll make you toss your cookies."

Reappearing, a grin on his face, holding something behind his back, Keith Klett moves close before Glenn where he sits chewing a mouthful of peanut butter sandwich. The others titter, giggle, offer expressions of sickness, as Keith Klett hangs near Glenn's face and sandwich a white rectangle of gauze blotched at its center with a blackish-red stain. Even as Glenn doesn't know exactly what it is, he has an idea and pulls his neck back enough, turtle-fashion, not to be touched by the daintily held object.

"Get out of here, Keith!" Gene Elliott says, adding to Glenn, to them all, "Anybody who gets a charge out of that has to be a pervert."

Not entirely certain of the function of the pad of gauze, Glenn decides not to ask. As Keith returns upstairs, white object in a pinch of fingertips, Glenn finishes his sandwich, drinks away his milk, and carries the glass to the kitchen sink where he rinses it out, as he does at home. Perhaps it has to do with his father's working second shift, leaving him to spend his evenings generally alone, or maybe it has to do with his not having brothers or sisters with whom to trade jokes and stories, but Glenn has a sense, realized for probably the first time, as he and the others are walking back to school, that maybe he is shy or maybe he doesn't have much that he wishes to say. It's a disappointing realization in its way, and he is disappointed too, in some attic area of thoughts, with the group of five which has decided to take him in. He had imagined something else. And a twinge continues in him over Rat Nose going off on his own. One thing Glenn does seem to see: He is a person. Each of them is a person, and each of them is different, and so is he, which is something he had never thought about before.

The season's first game is away, Friday after school. Lowell Junior High.

Thursday, at the end of practice, they are issued green satin trunks and white jerseys with green satin letters and numbers. Glenn will always remember that first digital identity, number 5, will feel a kinship with all who wear it. Cheerleaders and a bus load of students are scheduled to leave at three P.M. the next day, the Coach, clipboard in hand, tells them as they check the uniforms for size. Team members are to gather at the rear door at exactly two-thirty.

"You have a parent who can drive?" the Coach all at once asks Glenn.

"No," Glenn says, feeling that old rush of being from the wrong side of something.

"You don't—your mother can't drive?"

"I just live with my father," Glenn says.

"He can't drive?"

"Works second shift."

The Coach makes a mark on his clipboard, goes on to question others. In a moment, in the midst of assigning rides, he says, "Keep those uniforms clean now, and be sure to bring clean socks and a towel."

Four cars, including the Coach's own, will be making the drive, he announces at last. "Two-thirty on the button," he adds. "If you're late, you miss the game. And no one will change cars. Everybody will come back in the same car they go in."

The next afternoon, entering the strange school building across town, filing into a strange locker room, they select lockers to use and the Coach comes along, giving each of them a new pair of green shoelaces. Glenn—he rode over in the Coach's car with two other silent second-stringers—continues more or less silent now, sitting on the bench, removing his still-clean white laces, placing them in his gym bag, replacing them with the green laces. He also unstaples his second new pair of wool socks, thinking that later he will remove the new green laces, and save them and the second pair of socks for games only.

At last, dressed in the school uniform—number 5; he loves the number already and tries, unsuccessfully, to glimpse it over his shoulder—and new socks and bright shoelaces, he stands up from the bench to shake things out, to see how he feels. Nervous, he realizes. Frightened, although of what, exactly, he isn't sure. Goose-bumped in locations—along thighs, under biceps—where he has not known the chilled sensation to visit him before, he notices that one, and then another and another, all of them, have laced in the green laces in the stairway military pattern, while his make their way in X's. He feels himself a fool. Was there time to change? Should he say something?

The Coach holds up both hands. "Now I know you all want to play," he says. "Chances are you won't. Depends on how things go. One thing—I want each and every one of you to understand before we go out that door. You will listen to what I say and you will do as I tell you. There will be no debates. There will be no complaints during or after this game. Anyone who complains, about the game, or about teammates, or about anything, will find himself an ex-member of this team. Nor will there be any arguing with officials. No calls will be disputed. Remember: Losers complain and argue—men get the job done. They stand up to adversity. They win.

"Now, we're going to go out there and have a good warm-up. The starting five will be the starting five from practice and Ray Peaks will be our captain for this game. Now: Let it be said of you that you tried your hardest, that you did your best. Now: Everyone pause, take a deep breath.

"Let's go! Green and white!"

Throughout the warm-up, throughout the entire first half, in a continuing state of awe and shock, Glenn's goose bumps maintain their topography in unusual places. It is the first time he has ever performed or even moved before a group of people purposely assembled to watch and judge and count, and even as this occasions excitement in him, a roller coaster thrill, his greater sense, sitting on the bench in the middle of the second-stringers, is one of high-wire anxiety. His eyes feel frog-like, his neck has unforeseen difficulty turning in its socket, chills rush over his arms and legs.

From folded-down bleachers on this side of the gym only—opposite is a wall with high, wire-covered windows—Lowell Junior High students, teachers and parents clap, cheer, and shout as the game moves along. Glenn sits there. He looks around. His neck continues to feel stiff and sluggish. It occurs to him as he glances to the lighted scoreboard at the left end of the gym that he does not know how long the halves are. Six minutes and departing seconds remain in the first half, then, all at once, five minutes and a new supply of seconds begin to disappear into some tunnel of time gone by.

To Glenn's right, before the narrow width of bleachers next to the door that leads to their locker room, the cheerleaders from his school, half a dozen seventh grade girls in green and white, work, against all odds, it seems, to do their job:

Peaks, Peaks—he's our man!
If he can't do it nobody can! Yayyy!

Glenn does not quite look at the cheerleaders. He sits, elbows on knees, feeling self-conscious; carefully dressed, he feels he has gone to a dance of some kind when he has never danced a step in his life and would have declined the invitation if he had known it would lead to this. The seconds on the clock chase each other away; then, again, another fresh supply. Glenn looks to the action out on the floor without knowing quite what is happening. Nor can he entirely grasp what it is he is doing sitting here on the bench. Even as he went through the warm-up drills, he did not look at any of the spectators; rather, he looked ahead, or at the floor, or kept his eye on the ball as it moved here and there. How has it come to this? Where is he? His team, he realizes, is behind 17 to 11, and he could not tell anyone how this has come to pass.

No substitutions. As the first half ends and the Coach stands up, Glenn moves with the other second-stringers to follow along with the starting five to the locker room. Glenn feels no disappointment that he has spent this time sitting and watching, nor any urge to be put into the game. Sitting on the bench in that costume, getting his neck to swivel—it seemed contribution enough. As they pass before the group from their school, however, and names and remarks of encouragement are called out, he hears distinctly, "Go get 'em, Weasel," and looks over to see Rat Nose's face looking at him, smiling, pleased, and a pleasure of friendship leaps up in Glenn's chest.

The Coach paces and talks and points. They are behind 19 to 11. He slaps a fist into an opened palm. Glenn continues to feel overwhelmed by all that surrounds him, but at the thought of Rat Nose sitting out there, calling him Weasel, he has to stop himself from tittering and giggling out loud. For one moment, then another, it seems to be the funniest thing that has ever happened to him.

"Now we don't have much time," the Coach is saying. "We have to get the ball in to Ray Peaks. If we're going to pull this out, we have to get the ball in to Ray under the basket! Now let's get out there and do it. Green and white, fight—okay?" he inquires with some uncertainty.

On the floor, going through a confused warm-up, Glenn glances back at the group from his school, looks to see Rat Nose there in particular, but the group is too far away and at such an angle that he cannot be sure. Then they're being herded back to their bench; maybe they aren't supposed to warm up for the second half—no one seems to know.

Glenn sits in the middle of those on the bench and stares at the game as before. Five-on-five, two officials in black-and-white-striped shirts. Whistles. The scrambled movement of basketball at ground level.

Hands raised. Shouts from the bleachers. Yet again he has forgotten to check the beginning time. Nine minutes, thirty seconds remain as he looks for the first time. The score? His next realization is that he has not been keeping score. He is too nervous for math, he thinks. Home 25/Visitors 16. The next time he looks, the clock shows eight minutes, forty-four seconds. His team, he realizes, has scored but five points so far in the half. The other team's lead is increasing. It looks like his team is going to lose. That's what it looks like. There is Keith Klett snapping a pass to the side to Gene Elliott as they move before the scrambled concentration of players at the far end and Glenn experiences a vague sense that they are somehow progressing in the wrong direction, and he experiences a vague sense, too, of hearing his name called out: "Whalen—Whalen!"

It is his name, in fact, and there is the Coach's face as he looks, his fingers indicating sharply that he is to move to his side. The next thing Glenn seems to know, as if he has received a blast of frozen air, is that he is crouched, one hand on the floor, next to the Coach's knee. In this location the volume of the game, the cheers and spectators, seem to have increased three times over. "Check in at the table, next whistle, for Klett. Get that ball to Ray Peaks!" Glenn hears, sees the Coach spit the words at him from the side of his mouth, all the time continuing to watch the action at the far end.

Stealing along in the same crouch, Glenn reports in over the table top, says, "Whalen for Klett—I mean number five for number seven."

Taking a duck step or two to the center line, Glenn looks up to the scoreboard. Home 27/Visitors 16. Seven minutes, thirty-one seconds.

A whistle blows out on the floor and at once a horn honks behind him, giving him so sudden a scare he seems to lose some drops in his pants. "Substitution Emerson," the man calls.

Glenn moves onto the floor, into the view of all, seeking Keith Klett; spotting him, he says, "In for you," and believing he is the object of all eyes, moves past him toward the end of the court where the other team is putting the ball in play, not knowing, in the blur of things, if it is the consequence of a basket or not.

Nor does he see Gene Elliott for the moment as, before him, an official hands the ball to a Lowell player. The boy passes it at once to a player who turns to start dribbling downcourt and Glenn dashes toward him and the ball, slaps the ball away, chases it, grabs it in both hands, pivots, looks to find his fellow guard to get rid of the ball, as he is poked in wrist and forearm by someone's fingers and a whistle blows sharply, close by.

"Foul! Lowell! Number thirteen!" the official snaps. "One shot! Number five!"

The players return, taking their positions. "That's the way! Way to go!" comes from Glenn's teammates.

He stands waiting at the free-throw line. The others settle in, lean, wait. He has done this a thousand times, and never. The ball is handed over. "One shot," the official says. Glenn looks to the distant hoop; he finds presence of mind enough to call up something of the endless shots in the church driveway, although the message remains elusive. He shoots, from the chest, as he had in the driveway, although they were taught in practice to shoot from between their legs. Hitting the rim with a thud, the ball holds, rolls, tries to get away to the side, cannot escape, falls through.

"Way to go, Whalen," a teammate remarks, passing him on the way down the floor. "That's the way," comes from another.

Glenn moves toward the out-of-bounds line again, toward the other guard, as the ball is about to be put in play. He looks over for Gene Elliott again, but doesn't spot him, as the ball is passed in, and the guard receiving the ball, more alert this time, starts to dribble up court as Glenn rushes him, explodes over him, somehow hits the ball as the boy swings it in both hands, knocks it loose, chases it, dribbles it once in the chase, looks again for his teammate as the Lowell player is on him, jumps, shoots—sees the ball hit the backboard, hit the rim, go through—and hears an explosion of applause from the other end of the gym.

At once he moves back in, pursuing the ball, as a teammate slaps his back, says, "Great shot!" and he hears his coach call out, "Go ahead with that press, that's the way!" and hears the other team's coach, close by, snarl to his guards, "Keep it away from that guy will you?" and hears Gene Elliott, inches away, say, "Coach says to go ahead with the press."

There he is, poised, ready, so thrilled already that his eyes seem aflame, as the Lowell players are all back down court and are taking more time. He glances to the clock: seven minutes, twenty seconds. In about ten seconds, he realizes, he has scored three points, which message keeps coming to him: that he has in about ten seconds scored three points, that it is true, he has, and it is something, it is all things, and everything he has ever known in his life is different now.

The ball is moved along this time. At the other end, in their zone defense, the other team loses possession near the basket, and players run and lope past Glenn as he circles back, and the ball is passed to him, and he dribbles along, eluding a Lowell player, passes off to Gene Elliott, sees Ray Peaks ranging to the right of the basket, and when the ball comes back to him—it will be his most satisfying play, one which is in no way accidental, no way lucky—he immediately fires a long one-handed pass, more football than basketball, hard and high, and to his amazement Ray Peaks leaps high, arms extended, whips the ball out of the air with both hands, dribbles at once on a pivot turn and lays it in neatly off the board, and there comes another explosion from behind them. And there is Ray Peaks seeking him out, grabbing his arm, hissing in a wild, feverish whisper, "That's the way to pass! Keep it up! Keep it up! We're going to beat these guys!"

The game progresses. Glenn intercepts a pass and goes two-thirds of the court to put in a lay-up just over the front edge of the rim, as they were instructed, and he scores two more free throws, to go three for three, bringing his point total to seven, but his most satisfying play is the first long, high pass, and the most exciting experience of the game is the fever which infects them all, especially Ray Peaks, who scores any number of added baskets on his high, hard passes, and Gene Elliott, too, who passes harder, as they all become caught up in the fever, including the Coach, who is on his feet shouting, clapping, waving, and the group from their school, whose explosions of applause keep becoming louder and wilder, until, suddenly to Glenn, both horn and whistle sound, and there comes another explosion of applause, and the Coach and players from the bench are on the floor, grabbing, slapping, shouting, for the game is over and they have won, and they know things they had not known before, and none can quite get enough, it seems, of what it is they have not known until this very moment.

As they move and are being moved toward the locker room, Ray Peaks is slapped and congratulated, and so is Glenn. There is the Coach, arm around Glenn's shoulders, voice close, calling to him,

"That full-court press was the thing to do! You ignited that comeback! You turned it around!"

The celebration continues in the locker room. The final score: Home 29/Visitors 33. Locker doors are slammed, towels are thrown around, there is the Coach congratulating Glenn again, slapping his shoulder, calling to them all, "That full-court press turned it around!" Glenn learns, too, in the melee, that only two players on his team have scored, he and Ray Peaks, seven points and twenty-six, and everything, all of it, keeps occurring over again for him as a surprise, and as a surprise all over again, and he lets it go on as it will, a dozen Christmases and birthdays combined, accepts the compliments, knows in some part of himself already that he is changed by what has happened, has been granted something, knows these things, and does not volunteer in any way that at the time he simply chased the ball because he was so confused by all that was happening around him that he did not know, otherwise, what it was he was supposed to do.

Monday it is back to school and lunch hour as usual. After school, though, as practice moves along, as they run through drills with the dozen or so alternates, there comes a time for the Coach to name squads of five, and the name Glenn Whalen is called to run out and join the first team, in place of Keith Klett, who is left to stand with the others. It is not something Glenn anticipated—is a small surprise—but as it happens the logic is not unreasonable to him. Nor is anything unreasonable to the other four, who congratulate him in small ways as he takes his place on the floor.

Keith Klett stands among the others, retreats, Glenn notices, to the back row. His eyes appear not to focus on anything in particular as he stands looking ahead, glancing around.

They come face-to-face after practice in the locker room. Glenn, sitting on the bench to untie his shoes, looks to the end of his aisle and sees Keith Klett staring at him. "You suck-ass," the boy says.

Keith Klett walks on. Glenn doesn't say anything. He sits looking that way for a moment and doesn't know what to say or do.

Nor does he see the other boy when, undressed, towel around his waist, he walks along the main aisle to the shower. He wonders if they will fight, there in the locker room or out behind the school, and although the prospect of everyone streaming along uttering "Fight, fight," excites and terrifies him at once—he'll do it, he thinks—nothing of the kind happens. The remark stays within him like a speck; it stays and stays.

At home that night he thinks of resurrecting his friendship with Rat Nose and the thought appeals to him, as if to return home after having been away. Then he wonders if Rat Nose might turn his back on him—who would blame him?—and he worries about it until the next day when he encounters Rat Nose near his locker in the hall.

"Still go to Jobe's Market?" Glenn asks.

"Sometimes," Rat Nose says.

"Wanna go?"

"I don't care—wanna go?"

They walk along the hall toward the door. There is no mention of a change of any kind and they move along as if nothing has happened, as if it is merely another day.

PLAYING FOR MONEY

As he walks, sideways, past the landlord's Buick Roadmaster in the driveway, a longing comes up in him. The car is big enough to live in, has four portholes ringed with chrome along each side of the hood. Its sidewalls are white as milk and its chrome teeth reflect the blazing sun from all angles. Covered with dust at the moment, too hot to touch, the big Roadmaster's power triggers in him a deepening summer desire to do something, to go somewhere. To be another person.

In time, while his father continues to sleep, he looks up and sees the landlord back the long celery-green car out to the street and drive away. When Mr. Lewis returns and is lifting a bag of groceries from the front seat, Glenn is waiting in the midday sun and offers to wash the car for a dollar.

"A dollar?" the man says. "Yeah, okay—dollar sounds okay."

Glenn likes washing cars and a dollar is the going rate. He does not know it at the time—he is fifteen—but what he also likes is doing a perfect job. He washes cars when he can, to pick up spending money, to have time stop adding up on him. When luck is on his side, he gets caught up in doing a perfect job. No spots, no water marks, no film left on the glass inside or out. Doing a perfect job can transport him into dreams that are something of the somewhere where he longs to be.

He also imagines igniting the dusty Buick's powerful engine and driving it, if only thirty feet, into the shade behind the landlord's house. Pail, rags, scrub brush ready, he fixes the landlord's garden hose to a faucet along the foundation and unrolls it to see if it will reach the grass. The hose reaches, just barely, and on the man's small rear porch he taps on the loose screen door.

"Water will help the grass," Glenn says. "Main thing—it'll streak if it's washed right in the sun."

"I'll move it," the man says.

"I can move it—you know."

The man looks right into him. "You're how old?"

"Sixteen—when school starts."

"Yeah, yeah, I'll do it. All I need is some kid run my car in a fucking wall he ain't even got a driver's license."

Glenn and his father live in the garage house at the rear of the landlord's lot. They have lived in one other garage house before this, one with a smelly kerosene heater, and being called some kid and having ½ as an address, Glenn knows by now, are a couple of the cards he has been dealt.

Shirt off, barefoot in the grass, he occasionally sends sprays overhead, creating flash-rainbows and cool spatterings on his shoulders and back. The car hisses when he first runs water on it, and he floods the body, to cool it down, before going at it with an old soaked T-shirt of his own, a panel at a time. At last, washed and rinsed, he will wring out the T-shirt repeatedly and pull it like a chamois over areas of dripping metal. He gets into it. Tires, windows, added buffing and interior will follow. Ashtrays, trunk and floor mats will follow that. He gets into it; making the car's metal shine is a dream within which he has begun to sail.

Scrub-brushing a tire, leaning into it with both hands, he hears his father say from the driveway, "Looks good, when you gonna do mine?"

Glenn walks over. His father has his lunch bucket under his arm, ready to leave for work. "Whatever he's paying you, it ain't enough," his father says with a faint smile.

"I said a dollar."

"That's what he gives you—well, you'll have a look in the shifty eyes of a cheapskate," his father says.

His father seems sober in spite of his words. At this time of day, on his way to working second shift at Buick Assembly, he wouldn't have been up long enough to have had more than a couple of drinks; as always, though, on even a couple there is something dangerous about him that makes Glenn uncomfortable. He agreed to a dollar and a dollar is okay. He doesn't want his father to knock, smiling, on the landlord's door and invite him out to the driveway.

Money hardly seems to matter anyway. Water sprays from the hose have let him imagine he is at a lake in the country, riding in a boat, diving from a raft into green lake water, and talking to fish rather than talking to himself here in the sweltering, half-deserted city. "I'll ask if I can use the hose and do yours in the morning," he says to his father.

"Well, we'll see—better let me do the asking."

"I could do it before you went to work."

"I'll talk to him myself," his father says. "Right now I have to get a move on. I put a couple cans on the table so you can fix yourself something for supper."

Glenn looks at his father's back as his father walks toward the alley and their small, square house, which is not much higher than the car. The pint thermos in his father's lunch bucket, he knows, might carry coffee or Seagram's Seven, or a mix of the two. His father's lunch. There might be an actual pint in there as well, in a paper bag, to be slipped under the driver's seat, into the glove box, the trunk, hidden in a tree near the parking lot. Maybe to be sneaked into the plant, even as it is a violation—if a guard on the gate happens to check—which can have a worker suspended or fired.

Glenn knows most of his father's drinking patterns. At the same time, in spite of the booze, he has gone on with his own life. So he tells himself. He does not dislike his father, rather he loves him, perhaps adores him, as some sons do. Glenn rarely makes friends, though, he'd have to admit, and never brings any of them to the apartments or garage houses where he and his father live. He goes to school, hangs out in town or at the park when school is out for the summer. He gets along okay. So he tells himself.

He is drying a window when he hears his father's Merc start up in the alley. It is like his father to work at GM and drive a V-8 Merc. Glenn looks over. As the car with its evil-eye windows rolls into view, his father gives a toot, as Glenn knew he would. Glenn cannot see into the car, but he waves his hand as if he had seen his father wave. He had not known anything was wrong, then the horn toot called up being alone again, seemed to say that his desire to do a perfect job had been keeping back all morning a childlike impulse to cry.

"Let's take a look," Mr. Lewis says when Glenn taps on his door and says he is finished.

Glenn follows as they circle the car. Mr. Lewis, he realizes, as the man touches places with a finger and looks at it, smells the finger once, is not looking to see what has been done right, but is looking to find things done wrong. Glenn sees how different Mr. Lewis is from his father. When Glenn polishes his father's dress shoes, which he often does on Saturday afternoons as his father drinks and dresses in preparation to go out and prowl, his father holds the shoes to a window for light and exclaims how new they look. Their agreed-upon price is two bits, but his father never gives him less than a dollar, or two or three, even a five spot when his drinking is that far along.

"Okay, not bad," Mr. Lewis says, pausing, removing his wallet. "Wha'd we say, a buck?"

"That's right," Glenn says, surprised at the question.

Mr. Lewis crouches to glance at his reflection in a window of the car. Removing a dollar from his wallet, he extends it, folding it on the way—to make it look like two, Glenn thinks.

"Don't forget to clean up this mess," the short man says, waving a hand at the ground as he walks away.

"Don't worry," Glenn says, although not quite defiantly.

He makes a decision to roll the hose undrained, even though he knows better. He carries it ends-up to the landlord's porch, to let the water seep out where the man will have to step over the puddle, and in the process, Glenn knows, will have something to say about the kid who lives in the garage house back on the alley. His father was right; he'd seen into the eyes of something—a cheapskate for sure, he thinks, and it occurs to him that praise is as good at times as having a dollar in your pocket.

Well, up his ass with a ten-foot pole, Glenn says to himself, returning along the driveway. Take your fat-ass Buick and stick it up your fat ass

next to your brains, he imagines saying to the man, smiling to himself
at last and thinking he is feeling better.

There is something sexy in the cooler canyons between buildings
downtown, where pigeons peck and an amount of litter lies about.
Glenn looks forward to that downtown feeling—especially when he has
some money in his pocket—although today is just another summer day
and he has no more idea now than he did earlier of what it is he is
looking for. He counted his money on the walk down—sixty cents and
the dollar—and wonders, as his father sometimes remarks, if it is burning a hole in his pocket. Downtown can be a magnet, although he
rarely has the kind of dough he'd really like to have. Some days he feels
a desire to go to the park and shoot practice shots again, to resurrect his
basketball dream, while other days he feels the desire which is stirring
in him now, to be here in the midst of twenty-four-hour movie theaters,
of glass bricks and amber lights of forbidden cocktail lounges, even of
ice cubes in iced tea glasses in luncheonettes where middle-aged women
sit at small tables and hold high their skinny cigarettes.

At Playland, there in the skids of lower downtown, there are games
to play, one especially, a glass case wherein for a dime a mechanical
woman with pointed, black-nippled breasts and a headband like Wonder Woman boxes a mechanical man who wears tights and an old-
fashioned black handlebar moustache. Playland itself is run by a
seventy-year-old blonde whose lipstick defines lips she seems never to
have possessed and a man, her husband, one of whose front teeth is
gold, and who has threads of hair over his bare skull and a never-ending
scowl. Playland sells sneezing powder, trick matches, make-believe dog
dung, playing cards of pinups, and offers coin-games which are vaguely
dirty. The problem Glenn has with Playland is the feeling of being seen
entering or leaving. He enjoys himself when he is inside, feels excited
in a way, but he knows kids whose parents will not allow them to go
near the place, knows churchified kids who claim the decision not to
enter is entirely their own.

In lower downtown he might also park on a stool at one of the
half-dozen Coney Islands, have a hot dog smothered with chopped
onions and chili sauce and watch the world go by out on the sidewalk.
Or, on the bridge, tracing the warm caramel smell in the balmy sum-

mer air, he might buy a box of KarmelKorn. And a bottle of root beer. Or two bottles of root beer—tall dark Hires, which has become his drink—one with the Coney and one with the KarmelKorn, even though it would take all his money and he would be broke again.

Or—even if he is not yet old enough—he might shoot pool at one of two pool halls in lower downtown. He could buy cigarettes, move around with one in his lips and shoot imaginary games for money, straight pool, nine ball, eight ball, games in which he makes believe he doesn't miss even when he does, games—another of his secret dreams—in which he wins that commodity that always promises to make things okay, a wad of actual folding money. Or, he might walk uptown a few blocks to another pool hall—a subterranean cavern where various gangsters, hoodlums, and high school boys hang out—and see if he might run into someone he knows.

Glenn has circled the green tables often lately and his shot with a cue is coming into its own. Several weeks ago, on a Saturday night, his father, dressed in a sharkskin suit and a little juiced to be sure, spent an hour with him at AllSports and showed him some technical things—an appropriate way to use his eye, how to relax the hand guiding the cue, a lighter touch—and it was a breakthrough for Glenn. Almost at once his game was twice, three times as good as it had been. Times followed when he might run six, eight, ten balls, and ever more rarely did he have to make believe a missed shot belonged to the imaginary person whose clock and wallet he was steadily cleaning.

His father told him, too, of a legendary pool hustler out of Jefferson City, Lefty Withers, who had once made a living in towns along the Missouri River. The man's secret, even when he was well known, his father told him, was that he made it look like he had been lucky to squeak out a win. People would think the next time they'd get him, then he'd squeak out another win. He'd let them come close, his father said, and they'd keep coming back like suckers along life's midway who thought luck had something to do with things.

It was a new world of talk with his father—who treated him just about like an adult—and Glenn told his father in turn of a couple pool shooters who worked the pool halls in their own city. One was a colored man, Henry Little, who hung out at Capital Recreation, the underground world further uptown. Henry Little had great long fingers,

Glenn told his father, black on one side, pink on the other, and what he did was hang around the pool hall and challenge businessmen who stopped in at lunchtime and thought they were pretty good.

"Short games, I bet," his father said right away.

"Well, yeah," Glenn said. "Usually pretty short."

"You see—sounds like he puts on a show," his father said. "That's not the way to do it. Might impress you kids but he probably makes about six bits and the game's over."

"He always wins, though," Glenn said.

"That ain't hustling," his father said. "That's more like whoring."

Not quite knowing what his father meant by whoring, Glenn tucked it away. "Guy who's really the best shot of all plays at T. J. Halligan's," Glenn said. "Name's Sandy Solomon and he only shoots straight pool. I don't know if they play for money or not."

"Oh, they play for money," his father said. "I know who Sandy Solomon is—I've seen Sandy Solomon shoot a few games around Chevy Corners."

"You have?" Glenn said, pleased that he and his father had this in common. "I've seen him run forty, fifty balls without missing. The more he makes, the quieter it gets."

"I've seen Sandy Solomon do that," his father said. "There's an upstairs pool hall at Chevy Corners where he plays some of these guys. They play for money, though, you can be sure of that. Sandy Solomon. Bill Kennedy. They got the kind of class they don't try to put on a show like that colored fellow you were telling about."

There now, at work under the lights, are the long fingers Glenn had described. Standing in shadows to watch, he realizes how much admiration he feels for them nonetheless. Nor are they pink on the inside, as he had said, but beige.

On the thought—the sudden anticipation in fact—of seeing a game for money, maybe even being in one, he had turned away from lower downtown and headed uptown to The Rec, and found this game in progress. Whatever his father meant about whoring, Glenn's thought is that he'd still give anything to have fingers like that. The ring, too, on the little finger of the man's bridge hand—filled with apparent rubies and diamonds—which sparkle under the light.

His father was right about the amount of money, though, for after but one more game the two white men say they've had enough. As Henry Little suggests they shoot a game for time, one of the men tosses a dollar on the table and says, "That oughta cover it," and Glenn has the uncomfortable feeling that even though Henry Little won and doesn't have to pay for time either, something else has taken place.

Glenn steps over, drops coins into a machine, and pulls the knob under Camels. The package, three pennies along the side, and a book of paper matches fall into the trough. He hadn't quite meant to buy cigarettes, and does not know why he changed his mind. If he is going to go after his basketball dream in high school in the fall, he knows he should get off butts altogether.

As Glenn returns to where he was standing, Henry Little is unscrewing his cue stick and placing it in its case. He has checked in the box of balls to conclude time on the table, and slipped on a stained, blue pin-striped suitcoat he always wears, and as Glenn stands and smokes a cigarette, he sees the truth of something else his father said about Henry Little. Sandy Solomon—and the other white men who shoot straight pool at T. J. Halligan's—they all dress like they're schoolteachers, or bankers. Nobody passing them on the street would guess that one or another of them might be that most admirable of creatures, a wolf in sheep's clothing.

Still, he thinks, it's hard not to admire the great long fingers of Henry Little, who is just then coming his way. Henry Little winks.

"How's it going?" Glenn says.

"Got a smoke?"

"Sure," Glenn says, pleased to give a Camel to the celebrated man. Pack in hand, trying to jump one up, he has at last to pull it loose with his fingers. Striking a paper match, he cups it for Henry Little to catch a spark.

"Cain't make fifty cent 'round here no more," Henry Little says, taking a sizeable drag, standing there with Glenn and looking over the rows of tables, nearly all of which remain dark on this warm summer day.

"Everybody knows you."

"S'pose," the man says. "Wanna shoot a game?"

"Me? You think I was born yesterday?"

"Shoot, you ain't so bad. I seen you play; you goan be a stick one a these days."

"Don't have enough to shoot for money," Glenn says, thinking Henry Little might play for the fun of it.

"Make some scratch, you know, you got the scratch you need to make some scratch. Get the other guy to pay time. Always shoot a game for time, y'know."

Glenn exhales, tries to think of something else to say. He feels self-conscious standing with a man who is both celebrated and colored. "Yeah," he says, too loudly.

"Ain't even old enough to be in this place, is you?" Henry Little says.

"Almost," Glenn says, nodding toward the white-haired man, Jake, at the counter. "He never says nothing."

"You how old?"

"Fifteen."

Henry Little pops with wonderful laughter. "Shoot, man—see you around," he says. "Thanks for the butt."

Glenn feels good in the wake of talking and laughing with Henry Little. He almost feels like somebody. In feeling almost like somebody, however, it occurs to him that he often feels like nobody. What is he doing here anyway, he wonders, besides dreaming of himself as this person and that person? Winning this and winning that? Where his father works they produce Buicks; he produces dreams. What good are you, he wonders, if all that comes off the assembly line in your head are dreams of winning money?

He circles to the section of the underground world which contains the billiard and oversized snooker tables. Henry Little, talking to the shoeshine guy, T-Man, pistol-points a forefinger in passing, as if they had not just been talking. Glenn feels again, for the moment, that he is known to others, and it is almost a good feeling.

Next to T-Man's two-seater shoeshine platform a doorway leads into the pool hall's underground lunch counter where Glenn pulls up on a stool and orders a bottle of Hires. To the left of the counter a hardly recognizable hallway leads to a door marked PRIVATE. It is a card room, off limits except to members, and the men who pass on their way to the secretive interior are middle-aged and older, although a few may be in their thirties, and none ever shoots pool or is colored. They come underground from the marble-floored Capital Arcade, an interior mall of marble walls and small fancy shops, cross between the rows of pool tables, enter the lunch counter, and disappear behind the marked door.

In time, one or another of them comes out and walks away. Richer or poorer, who knows? Their faces say nothing. Many are Assyrian, Syrian, Lebanese, Greek, some are Jews—all seem to be gangsters—and few if any are factory workers although eighty percent of those who work in the city work, it is said, for General Motors. None are like Glenn's father, who migrated north a couple of decades earlier to find work in the burgeoning auto industry. None are hillbillies.

Sitting at the counter, Glenn sees Abadeen Leo Abadeen pass on his way to the card room. Maybe forty, Abadeen Leo Abadeen once lived up the street from where Glenn and his father lived. One thing he has is money, everyone says, and he is famous for driving a white Cadillac convertible, wearing silk suits—rumor has it that he runs a prostitution ring made up of white girls from Central High School—and is seen at night, by Glenn among others, driving by on downtown streets with one or another bleached blonde at his side. Another story has it that when shouts came from half a dozen high school football players standing on a corner, Abadeen Leo Abadeen pulled over and parked, turned off the Cadillac's lights and motor, stood up from a flashy blonde sitting in the car, removed his suitcoat, walked back and took on all six, was the last one standing, and returning to the car, took his time wiping his hands with a handkerchief and slipping on his suitcoat before sliding in beside the blonde and driving away.

"One thing about Syrian guys is they always have folding money and they know how to treat women," is a line repeated often in the pool hall. "They get the best-looking women and none of them would ever think of talking back or messing around or they'd get their teeth knocked in."

"Maybe they got something there, I don't know," Glenn's father remarked with a smile once when Glenn mentioned the Syrians. "You stay away from those guys, though," he said. "Those are tough guys and I'll bet every one of them's got an ace in the hole that'd catch you off guard and put you right on your ass when you least expect it."

Glenn does not fear for himself but fears, oddly, for his father—as in a bad dream—although his father has no relationships with such men.

His father has his edge, though, his pride, a swagger in his drinking and in his muscles and curly hair, his V-8 Merc, his three-piece suits, and his chasing around. That certain danger in the things he says. His father came home once with a black eye, another time with a swollen broken lip, and Glenn has a fear of him responding to some insult and turning to take them on, having little idea himself how money talks or how brutal they are and that they own the city.

The nine-ball game starts accidentally. Glenn is near the pinball machines again when a boy he knows only slightly comes along and bums a cigarette. Denny Leach is the boy's name and most of what Glenn knows of him is that he is eighteen and is called The Leach. He is someone to talk to and they stand looking over the empty tables, puffing Glenn's cigarettes. As if the person were Willie Pep or Roger Bernard, Glenn remarks that he saw Abadeen Leo Abadeen go into the card room.

"Owns part of the Tigers," Denny Leach says.

"Detroit Tigers?"

"Not in his name, in someone else's. Part of them."

"What's he own, a catcher's mitt?"

"Joke, asshole. Those guys hear you joke like that they find you floating in the fucking river your throat cut ear-to-ear, man, I kid you not."

Glenn thinks to joke about this, too, but lets it go.

In another moment two boys pass before them carrying a box of balls and a light goes on over Table 5, reaching out to contain the field of brushed green felt. The boys are brothers and Glenn knows them slightly, although they go to one of the city's parochial schools. Jim and Richie Carr. The younger, Richie, is Glenn's age; Jim, lifting the balls two at a time, placing them like eggs on the table, is a year or two older.

"Let's get into that game," The Leach says. "Come on, we'll win a couple bucks."

Glenn follows; they approach tableside where Jim and Richie Carr are rolling cue sticks, checking heft and tips. All fifteen balls are in the wooden rack.

"How about some nine ball?" The Leach says.

"Get lost, Leach, you never got any money," Jim Carr says.

"Where you been lately, Carr?" The Leach says in turn. "Haven't seen you around."

"I been around."

"You still carry old ladies' groceries at Hamady's?"

"Least I work; more'n anybody'll ever say about you."

"Afraid to shoot nine ball? We'll split the time."

"Not afraid to shoot nine ball with you, dipshit, don't worry about that."

"Let's do it then, nickel dime—put your money where your mouth is."

"You too, Whalen, you wanna play?" Jim Carr says.

"Sure," Glenn says. "For a while."

"We were just gonna shoot eight ball for fun," Jim Carr says. "You got money, Leach, or not?"

"I got money," The Leach says.

"Let's see it."

"Let's see yours, what're you talking about? Don't give me that shit!"

"You got money, Whalen? Neither you or Richie is old enough to be in this place, and I bet you both got the same amount of cash in your pocket, which is about fifteen cents."

"I got money," Glenn says.

"Okay—couple games is all. Pay up after each game! Okay? I'll pay for Richie. Split the time four ways. It's okay, Richie," Jim Carr adds to his brother. "We'll take some bucks from these dinks, game won't cost us nothing."

"Double on the nine," The Leach says.

"Goddam right," Jim Carr says. "Double on the nine."

"Double on the five too," The Leach says.

"Your funeral, asshole," Jim Carr says.

The Leach and Glenn select cues and, lagging the cue ball one cushion lengthwise, mark the table with moist fingertips to determine the order of shooting. The last to lag, on a sudden thought, Glenn strokes the ball slightly hard, so he will shoot last. Maybe they'll screw up ahead of him in the first game, he thinks, or maybe they'll leave him the nine and the break for the next game. The break in nine ball, his father has told him, is money in the bank.

"I'm paying for Richie," Jim Carr says as he chalks to break.

"Jesus, man, didn't you just say that?" The Leach says.

"But he doesn't have to pay me," Jim Carr says.

"Jesus, break will you, shut the fuck up!"

"Split the time four ways."

"I can't believe this shit—break will you!"

As something in the exchange is funny to the brothers, so is it funny to Glenn. He notes a comfort the two have in being brothers. They do not equal two people somehow, but three, and it doesn't seem that either of them would know the feeling that Glenn knows of coming and going by himself.

On Jim Carr's short, piston stroke, the cue ball slams into the diamond formation, the balls scatter, and the game is underway. No follow-through, Glenn notes, and finds himself taken with a competitive urge he has not felt shooting pool before. Has to do with time he's been giving to dream games, he thinks. Let them bicker; he'll slip up on them, take their dough, and leave them in the dust.

To his amazement, the first game goes as he had anticipated, although he fails to seize the full opportunity. By the time his turn comes—Jim Carr has pocketed the five—only the eight and nine are left, but the nine is a cherry on an end pocket. Taking a slice of the eight, he strokes the cue ball gently, and kissing the eight the ivory ball rolls along to put away the nine on a tap and return off the cushion. The nine spotted, however, blocks his line to the eight, and Jim Carr ends up sinking both and winning the break for the next game.

"We're even," Jim Carr says to Glenn. "Leach, you owe me twenty cents."

"You owe me for your brother," Glenn says.

"Right, I owe twenty cents for Richie," Jim Carr says. "We still made money; come on, Leach, pay up, you fuckstick asshole."

The Leach pays up, twenty cents each to Glenn and Jim Carr. To Glenn, handing him two dimes, Leach says, "I get down, man, cover my time, okay?"

"Don't have that much money," Glenn says.

"Jesus, man, I'm talking twenty cents."

"You already out of money, Leach?" Jim Carr says. "What a creep you are. Jesus, man, go walk in front of a bus."

"Don't call me a creep, creep! Your break, man. Your rack, Whalen, and don't make it too tight."

After but one more game, fifteen cents to Jim Carr on a double five and the straight five, and a dime to Glenn on the nine, The Leach is a nickel short paying up.

"You're ahead, loan me a half," he says to Glenn.

"Any of that crap and we're out," Jim Carr says.

"What crap? What do you mean? You talk like a donkey, you know that."

"You owe for time, Leach."

"Up your ass, man. What do I owe, a nickel? You pay it—you make all that money lugging old ladies' groceries. I'm out—fuck all of you. Whalen, give me a goddam cigarette."

Glenn gives him a cigarette, does not know how not to. He adds, though, "That's it," as he lights one for himself and holds the match for The Leach.

"Yeah, yeah," the older boy says, exhaling a cloud of smoke as he walks away.

"Still wanna play?" Jim Carr says.

"Sure," Glenn says, thinking he has the break coming and, fifty cents or so ahead, has little to lose, at least for a while.

Richie, who has said even less so far than Glenn, racks the balls, lifts away the rack. Glenn chalks up. Taking into account what his father told him about following through, he creams the formation and two balls go down, one of them the nine. The double credit on the biggest money ball goes through him like a shot; he calculated, executed, is already up forty cents for the game. He continues, and before he finishes his turn, adds the five; by the time the game is over, he adds the nine straight, and has the break coming yet again.

"Seventy cents," he says to Jim Carr.

"Thirty-five each," Jim Carr says.

Glenn only makes an expression to this, as Jim Carr is giving him the coins. "You're better'n you used to be," Jim Carr adds. "You been living down here?"

Glenn does not say. "Your rack, Richie," he says.

"Don't tell my brother what to do," Jim Carr says.

"His rack," Glenn says. "You tell him."

"Don't ever tell my brother what to do."

Glenn says nothing to this, but hair on his neck tingles. Thinking he will miscue if he puts his anger into his shot, he strokes lightly and, in a lesser clattering, nothing falls.

"Nice break," Jim Carr says.

He's working at pissing me off, Glenn tells himself. For even as it is obvious, he has never been the object of such a tactic in a game where anything like money was at stake.

Still, when the game is over, although Richie has made the five, the younger brother's only money ball so far, Glenn ends up sinking two nines and collects fifty-five cents and another break.

"Wanna quit?" he says to Jim Carr, not meaning it.

"Hell no, I don't wanna quit. I'm gonna win our money back. Your break."

Chalking to break, Glenn feels remote amusement, but also a touch of fear. He asked the boy if he wanted to quit to make him angry and it worked with surprising ease. He splatters the balls then and before his turn is over is up sixty cents and both money balls remain alive. For the first time in the game he feels he cannot lose. He is simply better, and when you're better, you're better. If he doesn't choke, he can't lose. The present game over, he adds a dollar ten to his winnings, a greenback this time, and a dime. He's won nickels and dimes before; this time, for the first time in his life—he can feel it—he's going to win some bucks.

As they continue, Jim Carr grows increasingly angry, while Glenn keeps focusing with added concentration, stroking ever easier, running two, three, four balls on each turn, racking up money balls at a rate of four or five of his to one or two of theirs. It comes home to Glenn that each shot he makes causes Jim Carr to tighten even more. He can't lose, he knows—not this time out—even if winning seems a distance yet away.

"Richie, hang it up," Jim Carr says in time. "I'll take on the pool room bum myself and get our money back."

Rather than being angered by the remark, Glenn feels sorry for Jim Carr, sees that he is making a fool of himself in front of his brother. Glenn takes a risk then, makes an offer he knows he shouldn't.

"Let's all hang it up," he says. "I'll pay time from what I'm ahead."
"No fucking way," Jim Carr says. "You owe me a chance to win our money back. And I'll pay our fucking time."

Glenn was going to walk to the counter to sprinkle talcum powder on his hand, but decides not to. He chalks his cue by standing it on the floor. "Rack 'em," he says. "My break."

"Quarter half," Jim Carr says.

Glenn stands there. He notices that Richie, who stands watching, appears frightened. It's getting out of hand, Glenn thinks, isn't at all what any of them expected. When he walked over with The Leach, rather than enemy to the two brothers, Glenn imagined himself as friend. "Okay," he says. "Quarter half."

Glenn's game only improves. He experiences added calm. Outside his ears there seems but a blur of sound. Within, between eyes and mind, a few simple gears seem to function with ease. There are the balls. Each time he sees a possible shot or two. Decisions are easy. He calculates, chalks, leans in. So much English, so much draw, so much cut or topspin. His bridge is steady, his stick hand relaxed. He strokes. Click clack. One ball rolls left, another angles right. *Plop.* Position is everything and more often than not, position is his. There's no way he can lose. He's going to destroy Jim Carr.

He chalks, circles, calculates. Outside his ears is a blur of sound, laughter, remote games. He looks down the cue, hefts the handle in two or three fingers, strokes. Click clack. *Plop!* He is doing it. He is hot. He is playing for money and winning big.

As another game ends, Jim Carr owes him two and a quarter. Short paying up, he turns to his brother. "Give me a quarter."

"You know I don't have any money."

Glenn stands there.

"I have my check from Hamady's," Jim Carr says. "I'm good for it."

"Let's just quit, Jimmy," his brother says.

"Shut up!" Jim Carr says. To Glenn, he adds, "Well?"

"Dad's gonna *kill* you," Richie says from the side.

"I said shut up!" Jim Carr says. Removing his wallet, he heads to the counter,

Glenn glances at Richie and to the boy his age makes an expression of sympathy or understanding. With the vaguest of sneers, however, the boy utters, "Screw you," and Glenn's heart drops, it seems, to his waist.

"Half dollar," Jim Carr says, returning.

"Nah," Glenn says.

"You won't give me a chance to win my money back?"

"I'm not playing double or nothing."

"Prick."

"You owe me a quarter for the last game."

"Add it to this game; I didn't get any change."

Glenn feels another risk coming up in him, and all at once he says, "Dollar two dollar," not knowing why he says it except that he remains stung over being called a prick.

The turnaround seems to confuse the other boy. "Okay," he says. "Okay! Dollar two dollar! Fuckinay, man! Dollar two dollar!"

"Rack 'em—my break," Glenn says. "You owe me a quarter."

"I know what the fuck I owe you."

Sighting down his stick, Glenn realizes that he is ready to attempt to slam the cue ball so hard the balls will explode, and in the midst of his emotion knows this is wrong. He can see the ivory ball airborne, hitting a wall. Back off, he thinks, and he stands upright, steps away, rechalks, studies the cue tip. Leaning back in, he looks down the stick, goes with a softer break, sees the five ball leave the pack, roll to the left-side pocket and drop cleanly, the only ball to do so.

Spotting the five, calculating his next shot, he says, "Two and a quarter."

The two brothers stand in the shadows in silence. Glenn shoots again, drops the one ball, chalks, studies, knows that nothing is going to change. "You can't beat me," he says.

No remark is forthcoming from the shadows.

Nothing changes. Glenn collects over three dollars for each of the next two games, and after another game, when Jim Carr owes him close to four dollars, the boy throws two bills and a nickel on the table and says, "I'm cleaned out."

Glenn's right pants pocket is stuffed with coins and wadded green-backs. He has won big, he knows that. He doesn't know how much, nor does he know what to do here in the face of the other boy being out of money. But he knows he has won big.

"Let's go, Richie," Jim Carr says. Looking at Glenn, he adds, "I'll have to owe for time but I'm not paying that asshole Leach's time. Richie, come on, goddammit!" As Jim Carr walks off, his brother moves to trail behind him.

Glenn stands alone. He has to take up the two dollar bills and the nickel from the green felt, and he has to take care of the table, although it is not checked out in his name. He has never won big before, and the feeling within him now, to his surprise, is closer to disappointment than satisfaction.

He feels unclean picking up the nickel. Why is it, he wonders, that his pride seems shaky and Jim Carr's pride seemed okay?

Forget it, he tells himself as he boxes the balls. Forget it. When you win, you win. You don't lose when you win. He carries the box over and pays the time. They played over two hours, and he doesn't mind paying time. A dollar forty-five. He pays by extracting bills and coins from his stuffed pocket, and turns to walk to the piss-and-disinfectant-smelling bathroom, to wash his hands.

The city remains warm even though the sun is near the horizon. Glenn crosses the street where there is little traffic—relieved to be out in the air—and walks in the direction of lower downtown. It's dinner-time and only a scattering of people and cars are around. Stores have closed; middle-aged men stand at curbs not to cross but to watch pass whatever it is that might pass on a summer evening. City air. It's downtown at an hour that he likes and he thinks as he walks that he is shaking off whatever it is that has gotten under his skin.

You won big, he tells himself.

At the US Coney Island, he sits on a stool near the windows and orders a Hires. Two other solitary customers are in the place, and when bottle and glass are before him he begins to remove his winnings almost secretly from his pocket. He presses grimy bills, stacks coins, counts to himself. Fifteen. Twenty. Twenty-five. Twenty-six, twenty-seven. Odd change. Factoring in the time and what he started with—no, he bought cigarettes and a root beer—he calculates that he won over twenty-eight dollars. Nearly thirty if Jim Carr had paid up, he thinks. He won big. It was what he had done, for sure, although he is trying still to call forth the feeling the money is supposed to have given him.

He leans along the counter to a jukebox console, thinking to play something that will move his mind elsewhere. He drops in a quarter and pushes letters and numbers. Often when he plays a jukebox he conceals his true selections in the midst of others, as if to conceal from some waitress a revelation of himself and his secret dreams.

Staring ahead, he waits. He hears a record turn into place within the mothership against the wall. He doesn't look that way; he looks to the street and wonders if the first song will be a decoy or the real thing.

From on high there comes a hum and Marty Robbins begins to sing for the three customers sitting apart in the summer evening's lull, looking wherever they are looking:

A white sport coat . . .
And a pink carnation . . .

Glenn keeps looking through the window to the street. The sun is below the horizon, and he sits hearing the music, looking away, and can see that he is on the wrong side of something, maybe of everything. This is what he can see.

Looking for a dream to get started, he thinks. That's what he's doing. Looking for a dream to get started, to have somewhere nice to go.

DRIVER'S ED

They are reading markers, looking to find their name chiscled in stone. They have gone up the long hillside, and back down, and are on their way up yet again in the part of the cemetery—if his memory of twenty-five years serves him right—where they should find the small gray stone and the plot of earth wherein, all these years, his father has lain unvisited. He keeps anticipating the moment—a shiver in his bones and heart, he imagines—of discovery.

His son, Dusty, to his surprise, seems caught up in the search. Dusty is thirteen and he was afraid, bringing him here, that he would be put off, even frightened, visiting a cemetery. "We'll just do introductions and be on our way," he told Dusty as they drove in and parked their rental car. "I'd just like you to say hello to this guy who is your grandfather—shouldn't take long."

It is taking long, however, but Dusty doesn't seem to mind. He pauses, reads markers, steps along and pauses again, fearlessly. Glenn does the same, twenty or thirty feet over. Dusty, he realizes, is more relaxed than he is himself. Well, he's far from home and there are no distractions, he thinks. Maybe, right now, as they keep winding along, Dusty is feeling the special fascination of history. He hopes so.

The sun, where they continue angling up the slope, is close and warm in the late March sky, although the air remains chilled in pockets and layers. The grass is matted yellow from the long winter; residue patterns on the grass look like lines of washed cigarette ashes. However quiet and peaceful the day, Glenn remains anxious, in fear of his son discovering the thinness, the tackiness, of where he came from.

"He won't talk back when I introduce you," he calls to his son. "At least I hope not—he always was full of surprises." Dusty glances, smiles, in the way, Glenn notes, of a person reading who would rather not be interrupted.

At the top of the slope, Dusty shifts to the next pathway in the sprawling low-rise community of stone and plastic flowers and starts back down. Glenn shifts over, too, to begin another sweep over the hillside. It's good, he thinks, that the maintenance shed was padlocked this first warm Saturday in March, good, too, that the cemetery offered no directory. All he wants, he reminds himself, is to have Dusty know that he descends from *two* branches of life, not just his mother's. Dusty's name is his name, after all, and is the name they are searching for here. Before today, though, he'd have to admit, he had rarely mentioned his own side of things to his children. He wasn't sure if he had ever spoken his father's name to his son. Clark Whalen—a man known as Red.

"How did he die?" Dusty asks.

Glenn's breath seems to pause as he looks over. "Suppose I take the fifth on that right now," he says. He and Dusty exchange a glance, but as he turns to resume the search, so does Dusty.

In a moment, merely to say something, Glenn calls to his son, "This bother you? Hanging out in a cemetery?"

"Not really," Dusty says. "Maybe a little at first—but not really."

Within another layer of cool air, Glenn smiles to himself as he imagines his father, underground, sending up the chill and grinning. The block of cool air appears in fact to have slid from a crevice just exposed to the sun. At the same time, something about it could be seen as unexplained, Glenn thinks. If one chose to see it that way. Green and red tree buds hang close here, no larger than peas and beans, and the blond grass is thinner, too, and more soggy, and Glenn wonders again, as he tries to determine the physics of its movement, about the origin of the block of cold air.

Red Whalen, he says to himself. Jesus. Watch his hands, he reminds himself. Watch the smile in his lips, the glint in his eye. Watch everything about him, and still miss something, and watch him grin, too, as he refused, no matter what, to give his secret away.

"*When* did he die?" Dusty calls over.

"Oh," Glenn says. "Over twenty-five years ago. I was fifteen. October," he adds.

Dusty appears to take this in as he resumes searching. His son's curiosity *is* stimulated, Glenn thinks. For better or worse. Glenn moves along, too, reads names and phrases carved in stone. Husband, wife; mother, father; son, daughter. Many are *Beloved*; a mother is *Adored*. Life and love are in the air, even as they are arrested in chiseled words and in the certain silence. It's a wonderful silence, he thinks. His heart is aroused at the thought, and he wonders if Dusty's heart might feel such a call, too, or if it remained impenetrable in its newness?

Stirring in Glenn again is his worry over presenting his past and his family, such as it was, to his oldest son. Alcoholism. Suicide. His own problems with the world, with the police in particular—two stays as a teenager in a juvenile detention center, one for only a few days, but the other long enough, over seven weeks, fall into winter, to never be entirely forgotten. Perhaps his growing up wasn't so extreme or unusual in some grand view of things, but he wasn't sure if Dusty would see it that way. Maybe it *was* extreme, Glenn thinks. Those years, in fact, had been an ongoing mess of sleepless nights and fear, misplaced time, his father's hangovers and disappearances, their separations, as much worry and anguish, as much shame, as much hurt, it seems to him in this moment, as anyone might ever believe.

Still, he thinks—still, all of it was touched with love, too, and in that way it came close to not being lost altogether. Wasn't that why they were here? There were parts of it, in any case, he wanted his children to know, to even appreciate, to take unto themselves. His wife's father was a kind and generous man. So was his wife's mother, even if she was as nervous as she was kind. His own father—he knew without any doubt—was unique. However irresponsible, however much his father may have misspent his life, he was other than average.

"What's this fifth thing anyway?" Dusty says all at once above a row of flat-to-the-ground markers and a tossing on the ground—so it appears—of faded cut flowers.

Smiling over his son's question, Glenn says something about a person not having to incriminate himself. And, as before, he remarks to himself that, well, the outing is working out okay. Dusty—as he should have known—is going to be fine in this unusual experience, maybe even wonderful in his way. His children often surprised him in their capacity to be wonderful. Children can be like that, he has told friends who are childless and occasionally curious. In the same moment, though, his thoughts run to his time in the army, when, volunteering little about himself, he would listen in certain fascination as others told, bragged usually, of friends and family at home, and he wonders what Dusty might say, away, of his home and family.

He wonders too, again, if what is in store here will upset his son. His old man's ragged—well, shameful—past. His own embarrassing adolescence. Three years in the army. That or wasted time in Boys' Vocational School. Might Dusty back evermore into the affluent arms of his wife's family? His wife's ever-embracing, gift-giving family. A certain risk, he thinks. No matter how Dusty might react at the moment, it was in fact a certain risk. Didn't every kid want Ted Williams for his father? or Czar Nicholas II? Even Abbie Hoffman? Who—wanted this?

Before Glenn all at once is not *Clark Whalen* but *Charles Wallis* and the name is close enough that his heart feels checked yet again. Composure regained on a pause, however, looking to see that Dusty is proceeding, he moves on.

A different anxiety comes up in him then. However warmly pleasant both the air and certain memories, he is feeling again that which he had managed over the years to keep out of his system: the old heartache, the perpetual uncertainty of living with a man whose closest companion, in truth, was a bottle in a paper bag. He should have known as this visit started that the old hurts would say hello. Heartache all the time. Never knowing what to expect—while always expecting something. Lying awake in bed at night, listening with his ears and with his stomach, too, somehow; sitting at a desk in school while a teacher spoke of Teddy Roosevelt and the Bull Moose party, where, as anywhere, the possibility always existed that his father, in some stage of drunkenness, might suddenly appear, that he might be funny, even eloquent, and other children might laugh and seem to like him. Or he might be so strangely drunk children would pull away from them both in confusion, or terror.

Red Whalen. His father was a speck of something in his eye always. An old nail in his heart.

Yet, in the worst drunken states, he remembers, his father proclaimed, expressed his love for him, begged him not to hate his old man. He hugged him, carried him on his shoulders, kissed his face, his hair, gave him too much money (asking later to have it back), asked to hear of every pitch of a game, every bounce of a ball, every word and shove. And when he was sober, or just a little high, and took him for a ride in the car or to the store to buy groceries or to buy him clothes or school supplies, or came outside to play ball with neighborhood kids in the street, there seemed no better father anywhere, and in pride and pleasure at those times, he had adored him. It wasn't what was carved into his stone, he knew, but it might have been:

Father
Unpredictable
Irresponsible
Sometimes Adored
Died Way Too Young

"My father shot himself," he says as he and Dusty near the end of another avenue of stone and brass markers.

"What do you mean?" Dusty says.

"Just what I said. He shot himself. Committed suicide."

"With a gun?"

"A rifle. It's awkward, I know. But it's what he used. I believe it was because a rifle could be purchased without going through a waiting period. Unlike a pistol. Although he did try it once with a pistol."

Dusty has stopped walking. "Where—" he starts to say.

"Where did he shoot himself? In the heart. Is that what you meant?"

"Yeah," Dusty says.

On Glenn's lead, uncertainly, they move along again.

"Why . . . ?" Dusty says.

This, too, stops him. "Why?" he says. "Well—lots of reasons. He—had a real drinking problem. I guess he was quite unhappy. You know?" It's almost a question, and although Dusty doesn't reply, they continue moving.

"We lived alone together at the time," he adds. "In that second-floor apartment I pointed out—that old green house, on the hill near the Buick plants—near the stadium."

Dusty may or may not remember the house, he thinks. Nor did it matter. In their rental car, before driving to the cemetery, he had pointed out a dozen or more apartments, rooms, small rental houses (all at once, in shame, glancing at it silently, he decided not to identify a converted two-car "garage house" in which he and his father had lived for nearly two years) and any number of schools, streets, playgrounds, diners, movie theaters, pool halls and street corners that had been background music to his unsupervised, delinquent childhood. The houses then as now were covered with dung-brown or blackish-red artificial brick siding—Insul-Brick, it was called—or with a slate composite, white or dull mustard or washed-out green, and all of his old neighborhoods were now black neighborhoods, doorless, windowless, lifeless ghettos even as they were approximately populated with scowling black faces, anger, heads belted with handkerchieves.

Pausing before the house where his friend Jobie had lived, he saw a black child in the doorway and heard the child call in alarm, if not in terror, "Momma, they's white man in a car!" He drove on, fearing some kind of hopeless misunderstanding. Still, he wanted to say to the child, "I lived across the street here! I grew up here! That's Jobie's house!" And he wanted to argue with the mother for putting into her child such fear of a white man.

There are, between Glenn and Dusty, some shiny new green plastic shrubs, with red plastic flowers, and the silence of the cemetery speaks to him again as it did earlier. Shame, he thinks. That was the real demon. Shame, in fact, had everything to do with why he hardly ever mentioned his family or his own past to his children. Stays in the detention home, hearings in juvenile court, probation and probation violated, arrests and rides in the backseats of police cruisers (was he arrested eight times? ten times?), until his father finally fired that certain rifle shot, and he left high school at last, a year early and two and a half years behind. A hopeless predicament, or so it seemed. But a GED diploma, and a turnaround, a good time in the army—the army was good to him and he liked nearly all of it—and work and college, and more work for a couple years, and marriage and graduate school, and a new life in the Northeast as, of all things—at last—an assistant professor in a state college (who, back in this part of the world, would believe it?), even if he was six or eight years older than most of the other assistant professors.

What a curious feeling shame is, he thinks. The feeling came up, he realized, every time he took in the plastic flowers placed here and there. Still, he thinks, at the same time that he feels ashamed he feels something like pride. Maybe just to be here. To have survived, to have worked his way out of the clinging past. All kinds of people pull it off, he thinks, including many whose childhoods were greater disasters than his own. What he really wants from his son, he realizes, is reassurance. Love and respect, and reassurance. "My old man's childhood was tough, but he survived it," he wants his son to say to his friends when he is away from home. "The odds were against him and he overcame the odds. He's a smart guy, my old man."

Is that why he is here? he asks himself. To confess who he is to his son?

"He was always, oh, sort of out of sync as a factory worker," he says when, without success, they have exhausted a full sloping side of the cemetery. "He was—devilish, if you know what I mean. A fancy dresser, a smile on his face, a light in his eye, you know, even though he was usually down on his luck, too, so he was kind of pathetic, and not your run-of-the-mill type factory worker." His uniqueness, he remarks to himself. He'll try at least to get across his father's uniqueness. The miserable parts, the drunkenness—maybe they were just as well left alone.

"What's 'pathetic' mean?" Dusty says.

"Oh—to be sad, I guess," he says. "At the same time that you might try to appear okay. That's what he was like—usually a little juiced, ready to tap his toes, ready to laugh. A rakish sort of guy, your grandfather. Although those are the good memories, to be sure. It's hard to remember the hangovers, and bad times—but there were plenty of those, too.

"There was always, for example, on the left side of his forehead, a lock or two of hair hanging out of place. Red—he was called Red. Red was more his name than his actual name, which was Clark. And he almost always had a cigarette in the corner of his mouth and, oh, a little

Mona Lisa smile on his face, in his lips. You would have liked him,"
he adds. "For sure—he'd have been crazy about you."

"Why did you say he did it?" Dusty says, his look and curiosity quite
real this time.

"That's hard to say," Glenn says, glancing over several shoulder-to-
shoulder brass veteran's markers. "Maybe I'll have to circle some more
on that—let it come up on its own . . .

"Besides being a fancy dresser—did I tell you that, that he was a fancy
dresser? Three-piece suits, fancy shoes, wingtips—he looked like a diplomat, like the nation's representative to the Court of St. James or
something, when what he was, really, was an hourly rate factory worker.
Buick Plant Three.

"He was a fancy talker, too. He had a touch of the poet about him;
or maybe it was a touch of high rhetoric, which he was capable of
getting into when he'd had a few. I don't know if he was so smart, to tell
you the truth, or if it was the booze talking. I *think* he was smart. He
loved FDR—and Walter Reuther was a man he looked up to probably
more than any other. The Red Head Who Fears Nothing is what he
always said of Walter Reuther, so I can remember, in school, arguing
for Walter Reuther with kids whose parents were management and who
believed Walter was a bad guy.

"He was strong, too, physically," he says. "He had real muscles, even
at the end—a trimness and firmness about him—he was a working man
all the way but he was never a person who became bitter about life. He
was a pretty tough guy, really, and he was almost always high—high as
a kite most of the time. I expect in fact, however sentimental it sounds,
that he had that little smile on his face when he pulled the trigger. That,
I guess, is pathetic."

"Wouldn't it—hurt?" Dusty says. "To do that?"

"I don't know," he says in a moment. "I think it might be too much
of a shock to actually hurt."

"Gee," Dusty says then.

"At least I hope so," he says.

"What did you call him?" Dusty asks. "Did you call him Red?"

"No," he says, laughing at the prospect.

"What did you call him?"

He is having trouble saying, then gets out, "Pop," as the word's mere expression constricts him.

"What did he call you?" Dusty is asking.

He has to take a breath, as he tries to approach the word. A gasp escapes, until he utters, "Redsie—as no one has ever called me—" He looks to a marker then as if he is reading the name, while his mind races throughout past and present.

"One thing," he adds in a moment, "the nose-to-the-grindstone guys, they're doing things with their sons and daughters today—like we're doing this. We're alive, you know—it's no small thing. My father, well, unless he's getting vibrations through the ground—where the hell ever he is around here—he missed this part of life."

Realizing that in his talking he has stopped walking again, he looks at Dusty and sees that he has stopped, too, and starts walking once more, to restart the search.

"Where was your mother?" Dusty calls over. "What did she do?"

"Let me get to that, too," he says. "I wanted to say—when my father died—well, things had gotten bad for both of us at that time. I was sixteen—just turning seventeen—and it wasn't one of the high points in my life either, I'm afraid. Being a teenager, your home life all confused—it wasn't easy to begin with and I didn't help matters much myself, but—well, maybe that's something I'll circle on too—okay?"

They continue under the March sun, and he tries, against the wandering of his mind, to continue to take in the names on the stones. What to tell? What to say? He had spent his seventeenth birthday in the county juvenile detention home, and he had just come close to attempting to explain that part of his life to his son. There were so many factors, so many things to consider, he felt too rattled for the moment to try. He did not know if Dusty would understand. Dusty's life is so different—night and day compared to his own, he thinks. The kind of kid in Dusty's world that he was in his childhood—well, how would Dusty see it? The punks, the white trash, the extremely poor in Dusty's life were called grungies—hoodlum type kids, many of them, that Glenn saw around the school's side door when he dropped Dusty off to go in to dress for soccer, or to attend a school meeting, boys with cigarettes in lips or fingers and sneers on their faces for the balance of mankind.

Dusty, stopped, calls him over then, startles him out of his thoughts. It isn't his father's marker, however, but a Plexiglas bubble over a grave. Within, visible through an amount of condensation, are recent cut flowers and several toys, a Santa Claus doll, a plastic ball, a tractor. *Brian, Our Beloved Son,* the marker says; the dates reveal that the boy died four years earlier, at age six.

"They bring him Christmas presents still—those things are new," Dusty says.

Crouched, one hand on the ground, Glenn looks through the Plexiglas. "Experts say it's really hard to outlive your children," he says. "One of those irreconcilable things."

"One of *what?*" Dusty says.

"Something it's hard ever to leave behind," he says.

"Irreconcilable," Dusty says.

He smiles, standing. "You're pretty quick today," he says.

Dusty smiles.

"You can come to terms okay with losing your parents," he says. "It's natural. It's as if, as you grow up, you're supposed to arrive at that time of being on your own. Especially if your parents had a reasonable life in terms of length and happiness."

"What about your dad?" Dusty says.

"Well, your grandfather," he says. "I'm not so sure about him. I used to think—maybe he made up in intensity for what he missed in length. He did a lot of things, you know. Grew up in the Depression—which may be an explanation for his never being successful. He rode the rails, all that stuff, for real. He *walked*, he told me—several times—walked once all the way from near St. Louis to Chicago. Took him seventeen days, and he said it was one of the best times he ever had in his life. Grandpa in Vermont, not to take anything away from him—he's worked hard all his life, but, well, my father, he was a romantic, a kind of swashbuckling no-account who believed in things that were probably impossible, but kind of nice to believe in, you know?

"But I don't really think the intensity made up for that much," he says then. "Which is why we're here—looking for him. It's why it's strange to be here—for me, for you, too, I guess. His life is unfinished business, is what it is. It would be one thing—to stop here, put some flowers in the ground, say a word or two, extend a fond memory and go on our way. Which is what we'd probably be doing if he'd been some other kind of man. We'd have gone right to his marker, and it would be a reasonable chunk of stone, and we'd be long gone by now. Business completed; back to business at hand. Back to life as it rolls along. But . . ."

Standing there, both keep glancing at the Plexiglas bubble between them.

"Anyway, let's find him," he says. "We came this far. All I want is for you to meet him, then we'll hit the road. To meet me, I should say. Therefore yourself, too. That's what I guess I want you to do."

They move out again, a search party of two moving from marker to marker, reading names. The car they signed for the previous day at Detroit Metro—a Buick Regal—is downhill before them at the ruffle-edge of the broad slope of markers, at an angle now which indicates they have covered about two-thirds of the cemetery. Glenn sneaks another look at Dusty. Looks fine, he thinks, doesn't appear uninterested in this curious adventure, nor put off, it seems, by all the words being sent his way.

His excuse for taking his oldest son on this trip into his own past had been an appearance by their hometown college hockey team in the national playoffs at Detroit's Joe Louis Arena. The rental car, reserved and waiting at the airport, had been his planned escape from the plane-load of high-spirited hockey buffs. Not that he and Dusty were not buffs too, for they were. On cold nights throughout the snow-blown winter they had gone to watch a dozen or more games in the tension-, haze-filled college arena, and Dusty had become such a player of youth hockey that he had picked up a nickname from teammates—"The Duster"—for his tenacity in the corners as well as his shot. "Leave 'em in the dust, Duster!" friends would call out, and, "Here comes The Duster!"

The night before, when their team had lost, in overtime, and it was a sad end of a certain brief road, Glenn had been relieved that his companion on the trip was his thirteen-year-old son. He was relieved, too, that they could bypass the drunken remorse-revelry of the others, could slip away into the March night for a late meal together—pizza, extra cheese and pepperoni added to assuage their disappointment—and a walk under the star-lighted sky in the shadow of the Renaissance Center, pausing to study the lights of Windsor across the moon-reflecting water. He was relieved, too, that they could turn in for a full night's sleep and slip away in the morning while the rest of their group ate aspirin and dozed and were bussed back to the arena for an afternoon consolation game.

More of his aloofness, he thinks. The old charge. It comes to him for the first time, as he plods downhill, that this, too, might be an after-effect of the man whose remains they are trying to locate. Only as Dusty had grown old enough to join teams had it become an issue. There had been accusations, through slightly smiling lips, and whisperings, too, about what was called Glenn Whalen's aloofness. His wife—informed by other wives—had spoken to him of the problem and had urged him to try not to be so standoffish. Needing time merely to understand the charge, he ignored it—he had little feel on how to do otherwise—and continued to conspire to spend such occasions with one or another of his two sons rather than with other parents. His thinking, when he thought about it, was simple; he felt uncomfortable with one, enjoyed the other. Only now, however, as he is gazing at yet another family of markers, does it occur to him that another reason he chooses the company of his sons is that he does not like the questions that come from other parents. "Where you from originally, Glenn?" "Glenn, where did you go to school?" "Your father still alive, Glenn—what did he do for a living?"

This, he thinks, is how he liked to spend time with Dusty or his younger brother, Danny. Alone. What he liked especially, with either or both—he realized early on—were drives alone together along strange highways at dawn, the two boys asleep behind him as he drove along a two-lane highway. He also loved truckers' breakfasts together at unknown road-stop restaurants, loved above all the talk of things small or funny and real, at times the special silence of sitting over lukewarm coffee at daybreak at some outpost truck stop near the Canadian border in northern Maine or New Hampshire, trading sections of a rarely seen newspaper. This, he thinks. It was something he liked as much as he had ever liked anything. This.

The Buick Regal. He was considering a plan for that as well, one that had come to mind the day before when they slipped into the car at the airport and Dusty, noting the neatly marked automatic transmission handle, remarked, "I could drive this car." In that moment, Glenn decided, it was the car in which he would teach his oldest son how to drive. Before they returned the Buick, in a parking lot somewhere, or along a country road, he would pull over, put Dusty behind the wheel, and say, "It's all yours."

"Dad—do you believe in ghosts?" Dusty calls, pulling him back to the present.

"Oh, I don't think so," he says. "I don't know. If I ever thought anyone would put up a ghost, though, it would be this guy we're looking for."

"Your father—as a ghost?"

"He's related to you, too, you know. He's your grandfather. On my side."

"I never knew him, though."

"That's why we're here," Glenn says. "Anyway—he was always so full of hell, so full of the devil, it could be he became a ghost. He'd be a friendly ghost, though. I can't imagine, you know, his ghost being mean or anything. He'd tickle your ear or something—tie your shoe-laces together, drink your milk when you weren't watching. What he'd do," he adds, starting to laugh, "what he'd do is slip up and put down the right answer to some math problem so you'd have no choice but to think the dog had done it. That's the kind of thing he'd do."

"When you—" Dusty starts to say, but doesn't finish.

"What were you going to say?"

"You—when you die—you can't ever come back, can you?"

In a moment, in case it was a question, Glenn says, "No, you can't ever come back."

"Not even as a ghost?" Dusty says and this time, looking over, smiling a little, it is a question.

"Not even as a ghost," Glenn says. "At least so far as we know."

As they push on, he is asking himself again what to tell, what to say. At last he says, as he knows he wants to say it, "My mother was alcoholic, too, for that matter, but she was so long gone that what she was, was forgotten. By me, at least. Not by my dad, though. In fact, I don't think he ever really got over her. The truth is—I believe—the sad truth, is that he lived the rest of his life, after she left, looking for her and waiting for her. Which was our life together. His and mine. Unless he only used her as an excuse to drink more. I don't think he did. He was always looking for her. His whole life, after she took off, was a kind of drunken search, a waiting for her to come back.

"Which she did, a few times—which, I think, made a believer of him for all the rest of the time when she didn't. Ostensibly, she came those few times to visit me. My father always gave me money, though, and I'd go off to a matinee or something and leave them alone so they could drink, I guess, do whatever. I'd go to the park, you know, and practice my shot. Practice free throws. You know my free throws—that's where they came from. Daydream. I did a lot of daydreaming when I was your age, and I only had about one friend at a time, or none at all, and that, too, was a consequence of my father's drinking. What can I say—it's true.

"Once, when he'd had a few, near the end, he told me that every time he went to a bar he looked to see if my mother was there sitting on one of the stools. His fancy clothes—they were part of his waiting, part of his being ready for when she might come back or when he might find her and bring her home. Maybe his always being high was part of it, too, I don't know. She was a knockout, my mother. She was a lousy mother, though. Unlike your own. Otherwise, I don't know what she was like, because I hardly got to know her. She looked like a movie star—big eyes, a strikingly attractive woman. Anyway, the sharkskin suits and wingtip shoes—he'd come home from work; he almost always worked second shift, so I ran the streets a lot at night—he'd come home from work, change out of his denim coat and railroad hat, clean up, put on a three-piece suit, and go out haunting the bars, simply on the chance, I learned in time, that she'd be sitting on one of those stools, that she'd come back and they'd start life over again.

"When it got so bad, finally, when he had almost entirely drowned himself in the bottle—when it looked like I was lost to him, too—he killed himself. Put an end to the waiting. An end to the hurt he seemed always to feel."

Glenn stops again, is stopped by thoughts rushing up in his mind. "The truth is," he starts, but lets it trail off. No, not this, he thinks. Don't tell him this.

What is in his mind is an old thought that his father had in fact killed himself as a gift to him. The only gift he had to give, is what it had seemed to be, as if he knew that in trading in his own life he might set his son free, that he might give him some self-reliance, or purpose, besides.

They move along. Into new silence, he says, "People talk about how bad it is to have an alcoholic parent. What's worse, I think, is to have a parent who doesn't love you. Because then, I believe, you don't love yourself. Does that make sense? Well, that wasn't the case for me. Which is why we're here. It's not the case for you, either. If you know what I mean."

Dusty smiles, nods, doesn't quite look at him.

"Do you?"

"*Yes!*" Dusty says.

Glenn smiles this time.

They pause yet again, at the top of the next row, the last. It comes to him then, clearly. They are not going to find him. Just like that—he knows. As always with his father, he thinks, something is wrong. Maybe everything was always wrong. They will not find him. The sonofabitch, he thinks. He always did this to him. Perhaps he was evicted, removed physically, thrown out or away for bills unpaid. Maybe perpetual care, like life in prison, was reviewed after so many years. Could he have been discharged for bad behavior? Or—could it be—when all those years had slipped by and no one had stopped to visit, might he and his small stone have been removed, thrown away, his moment of life erased, his home in the earth given to another?

"I don't think we're going to find him," he calls over.

"We still have this," Dusty says, indicating the double row of markers still before them.

"I don't think he's here anymore," he says. "Unless they moved him."

"Maybe they did," Dusty says.

They continue in their final sweep. Glenn looks, forces himself to look twice at names, as his thoughts keep wandering. Here he is, trying to present his father with fondness to his son, he thinks, and feeling abandoned all over again. Who wouldn't feel aloof?

As they are approaching the last several markers, the last seconds in a game that is certainly lost and an empty feeling is coming up in him, he calls to his son. "How are you doing? You must be getting hungry."

Dusty doesn't answer. Glenn looks to read his last marker, and there, too, is Dusty reading his, and he knows all at once that his son is disappointed in their curious failure.

"He's not here," he says. "He must have run off somewhere. It's just like him."

Nor does Dusty respond to this and he knows from the angle of his son's eyes and from their lifetime together that he is hurt in a way.

They turn on the dirt road that leads to the car, fifty yards before them. Glenn wants to touch his son but is hesitant in this moment—the loss, after all, is in the name of his side of things—then reaches a hand around his son's shoulders as they walk along, and feels Dusty agree to the embrace and move with it.

As they near the car, he says to him, "Think you can really drive this thing?"

In half a second, Dusty's eyes widen. "Are you serious?!" he says.

Glenn smiles. As they turn to the driver's side, he removes his jacket, folds it as a cushion.

"Get behind the wheel, fix the seat, and the mirrors. Always do that in a strange car," he says. "What you can do," he adds, knowing he is sounding a little like his own father, "you can always say, all your life, that you drove for the first time, age thirteen, that your old man taught you how to drive along the dirt roads in a cemetery where you couldn't find your no-account grandfather's burial plot even though you knew he was there somewhere."

He is getting into it, into something unforeseen, he knows, as he moves to the passenger side. His own voice—he could be a little intoxicated himself—has surprised him. "I'm going to teach you how to parallel park so you won't ever forget it," he hears himself say. "People who can't parallel park disappoint me," he says. "They lose respect coming and going, and whatever you'll ever be, you'll never be one of those sappy types, I'll tell you that."

Oh, it is his old man—showing up after all.

"Otherwise," he adds, "you'll be teaching yourself. I know you know how to do it—how to use your head and work through mistakes. I'm going to keep my mouth shut and let you do it."

Vintage Red Whalen, he thinks.

"Here's the key," he says, and he thinks, too, as he sees the pleasure

Dusty is taking in being handed such a task, thinks and knows in this moment that the moments of slightly intoxicated daring were what he loved in his father. Slightly intoxicated, his father was fun, full of stories and affection, more fun than anyone ever and the only person with whom he ever wanted to be. They had such good times at those times; his father was so smart and they felt so good, acted with such daring, laughed with such pleasure. It's a feeling he relishes passing on. And when he adds, "We'll toot the horn at some point—a single toot—so he'll know it's us, one toot to say Hello father, grandfather, and farewell for now; we'll meet again, don't know where, don't know when," he isn't entirely certain whose voice is speaking.

Adjustments made, motor started, the car jumps, rocks, dips, jumps again before Dusty gets it rolling more or less smoothly on its way. Sneaking a look—eyes filmed—he sees Dusty stretching his neck to maintain a view over the steering wheel, sees how intent he is upon mastering the task.

And as they roll along, as they traverse and climb the broad slope, he entrusts all, turns over all to his son, this young boy he loves, imagines himself back at the foot of the hill watching the car move in pursuit of its ongoing intersection of things. And when the toot of the horn is given and calls out over the quiet slope of old lives, he takes it in, and it is reassuring to hear, it allows a glimpse, the heart shiver, the voice after all that he had been waiting to hear, as the two of them, the three of them, roll along the narrow road.

AN INTIMATION OF DEATH BY SUICIDE

Their car tires clatter over a long wooden bridge just above tidal marsh and shift to the sudden smoothness of blacktop. They roll on under a sky threatening rain mixed with snow, tracing this back road of New Hampshire in pursuit of the Maine Turnpike.

Glenn is driving his son, Danny, to one of his Saturday morning hockey games. An away game—outings Glenn has come to enjoy. Away from it all for much of a Saturday, this time to the arena in Biddeford. Just the two of them.

The radio is playing vintage music at low volume and they are playing a game Danny has invented called "Purely Pickups." The clarity of his son's game returns Glenn to better moments of childhood with his own father. So long ago, he thinks—although lately he has been remembering. A moment ago, on a glance at Danny, he saw himself as a twelve-year-old riding in the passenger seat, and he thought, well, one thing he won't be doing is asking Danny to pass him a pint in a paper bag as his father was always asking him to do. Nor will he careen hell-bent along the highway firing make-believe pistol shots from his window, calling up John Dillinger, Clyde Barrow, games of cops and robbers. Or have Danny sit on his lap and steer the speeding car. His father's pastimes, the pastimes of a drunk, he thinks; however thrilling they were to him as a child, he has never taken them on as his own.

Purely Pickups is a counting game. Ten vehicles passing belong to Glenn, ten belong to Danny. How many pickups in one's string of ten? The average is five or six, and occasionally an opening run of five or six has them anticipating a perfect score. Their all-time record is nine, and even as they occasionally reconsider the qualifications of a cutaway Bronco or a small dump truck, they always decide to count only true pickups. Thus did the game's name come into being.

Wet snow begins to hit the windshield and they drive with headlights on in the darkening midmorning air. The interior of their big vehicle, a Wagoneer, is warm and holds the snaking road in Quadra-Trac as they glide by clustered mailboxes and newspaper tubes, mud-rutted driveways, abandoned cars, blue-jacketed snowmobiles.

Danny wins a round six to four. Moments later he wins another—an opening six-straight run gets their attention—eight to four. As always they pull for the number to be high and the loser is not introduced to suffering. Stretches of light traffic allow moments of silence and occasions to speak of something else, and when they emerge from the backwoods to climb the ramp to the big divided highway, the game, as always, is left behind until another time.

"Goodnight, Irene" comes on the radio—Glenn turns the volume up a little as they enter moderate traffic on the turnpike—and the song comes up too in the apartments and garage houses in which he lived with his father long ago.

Last Saturday night I got married . . .
Me and my wife settled down . . .

A ghost out of the past. An old emotion. His father played the song over and over, and only now does Glenn seem to feel what he imagines his father felt then. Car tires on the turnpike throw up sprays that have him turning on the windshield wipers, as the song plays down through the years, and in his veins too, where it plays bittersweetly.

"Goodnight, Irene" was one of his father's favorites, but when it played at an early hour like this it meant his father had yet to go to bed and was drinking heavily. It meant—when Glenn was awakened in his bedroom to the record going around and around out in the living room—that his father was there or in the kitchen after having been out all night. It meant that his father was lost again in booze and despair, heartbroken with the failures and disappointments of his life. Resentful, sometimes dangerous. On the edge of sliding to the floor into sodden unconsciousness. And, near the end of it all, obsessed with suicide.

Drunk again. Life with an alcoholic. What, he wonders here, rolling along the Maine Turnpike, did his father's drinking do to him? All at once he wonders—all at once he thinks he'd like to know.

> Now me and my wife have parted . . .
> Gonna take another stroll downtown . . .

What to do when his father was drunk was always a question for which there was never an easy answer. A record going around and around and the intoxicated figure of the powerful man looming between him and an escape to school or playground or downtown—it happened perhaps a thousand times. Hiding in his bedroom, walking the streets at daybreak, leaning on the bridge railing over the river downtown, sitting on stoop or curb in the sun, sitting on a stool in a diner waiting for time to pass, waiting for his father to fall asleep or pass out, so he might return home.

School mornings were the most tense, and he learned to hate being late for school. He was unable to tell the truth and teachers did not believe his lies. Into the sauce, his father did not care if Glenn was late or not. Some lesson of mind or heart, a philosophical point, a declaration of love or the dramatic high point of a drunken narrative—his words, his father had no doubt, were more important than two-bit lessons of the classroom.

The songs were not played loudly, but the records were played over and over and Glenn became imprinted with them. Words, melodies, phrases entered his veins, are within him still, he is reminded here again, more than twenty-five years later.

> Sometimes I take a great notion . . .
> To jump into the river and drown . . .

His father let a record play fifty, a hundred, two hundred times, throughout a night, into another day. "Paper Doll." "Your Cheating

Heart." "Why Did You Give Me Your Love, Dear, When It Lasted Only a Day?" "Someday You'll Call My Name and I Won't Answer." "Cold, Cold Heart." Out of mind for weeks, any one of the records might be taken up again. At four or five on a Sunday morning there would be Margaret Whiting and Jimmy Wakely's "Slipping Around" slipping through the wall once more into Glenn's small bedroom, into his ears and heart, into him, to remain forever.

It's odd, he thinks as he drives, that he did not come to hate the songs. To the contrary. When one plays, as "Goodnight, Irene" is playing now, he is transported in a way that is deeply gripping. A sweetness of pain. The sensation is hard to understand. Nostalgia is hard to understand. He knows only that it is an emotion that enthralls him, is more wistful than sentimental, is immediate and as powerful as powerful words.

Did his father's alcoholism leave him an emotional cripple, too? Was that what had been done to him—and he had never stepped enough outside of himself to see it? Had seeds been planted long ago? Could he—as he sometimes feared—slip into a downward spiral and end up equally lost in emotional despair? It hasn't happened, to be sure, but he is not unaware of the nearness of a certain chasm. Homeless alcoholics on the street are more old acquaintances to him, for sure, than strangers.

Is suicide contagious? he wonders. He recalls overhearing a conversation between two women in a kitchen as they discussed a current unexpected suicide. "I feel sorry for his children," one of them remarked. "He was otherwise a good father and suicide like that gives the message that it's okay."

Glenn glances to Danny, notes how quiet he is as he studies the turnpike ahead through the windshield. He and Danny are both quiet and on drives will often roll along for miles without speaking.

"Whatcha thinking about?" he decides to ask the adored twelve-year-old boy who is his son.

Danny looks his way, says, "I don't know."

Glenn returns his eyes to driving, hears Danny say, "Alan hasn't paid his registration."

Glenn drives along. Alan Lebrie, a boy who lives on the edge of town and is extremely poor, is one of Danny's best friends, the only child of a native New Hampshire couple. "He's really late isn't he," Glenn says at last, referring to the unpaid hockey fee. "Lots of money, too," he adds.

He glances Danny's way, sees him gazing ahead once more through the windshield. He advances the windshield wipers as the wet snow is thickening, and increases the radio volume another turn, detecting another song of the lost days and nights of the past, "Born to Lose."

Glenn recalls a time when he had started seventh grade and he came to the end of some rope and nothing mattered anymore and he broke down and charged from his bedroom in confused cranky tears on his way to the phonograph where the needle-arm was starting around for perhaps the fiftieth time. His father's voice—he recalls it distinctly—said from across the room, "Don't touch that."

"I can't stand it anymore—I'm going to touch it—I can't stand it anymore!" he cried to his father, even as he was affected at once by the tone in his father's voice.

"Do, and I'll knock you on your ass," his father said.

Glenn did nothing. His father had never spoken to him like that, drunk or sober, and Glenn did nothing. He was not knocked on his ass but he was knocked off some perch for the first time, was crushed and tamed at once, and the tears that fell from his sleepless eyes fell in embarrassment and disgrace, in humiliation of a kind that only a child new to puberty seems to suffer. His father had always treated him with humor and kindness, and even if he did apologize before the long day ended—"It's those snakes that hide in whiskey bottles," he said, urged a handful of greenbacks on him too—his threatening voice was one Glenn had never been able to quite erase.

"Do, and I'll knock you on your ass."

The voice occurs again in his mind as the song on the radio makes a turn—one he knows so well—into its refrain.

. . . born to lose . . . and now I'm losing you . . .

Another morning, near the end, plays out in his mind. He sees himself move along a short hallway to a living room doorway. He was fifteen or sixteen. The apartment—it would be their last—was previously an attic and like his small bedroom, the short hallway had a slanted ceiling. The only exit was through the kitchen door and a fear was in him of being intercepted by the sodden figure and made late for school while he listened to a new, or old, motive and means for the ending of his life. He paused at the doorway. What was on the other side where the music played? Things broken? Weapons? Unconsciousness? Death?

The song was ending—Glenn knew each click and hum of the arm lifting-shifting to return and start over—as he peeked around the door frame.

His father wasn't in the living room. The phonograph lid was raised and a voice was escaping the dark speaker screen, crying out that a promise was all in vain, that a heart . . .

. . . keeps calling to you, dear . . .
Like the flowers call for the rain . . .

Peeking around the edge, Glenn could see that the swinging door into the kitchen was propped open, to facilitate, he knew, the music's sad journey into his father's battered heart. School was important to him this morning—maybe he had a report to turn in, or was scheduled to stand before the class and define photosynthesis; perhaps he was simply filled with an old fear of being trapped, of being the object of hurt and despair—as the signs indicated that his father's drinking was on its way to a new disaster. How to escape? How to get away—out into the air?

In the living room, calculating—he'd have to take up his books from the kitchen table on the way through—he slipped on his jacket. He envisioned his father guarding the exposed wooden stairway down the rear of the old house and his thought was to be ready at the first opportunity to exit, no matter breakfast or hunger, no matter how early it might have him on the street with time to kill before school began.

The man stood in the kitchen, head hanging, eyes closed. Was he unconscious? His back near the counter, his chin sagged to his chest. Could a person be unconscious on his feet?

Life with an alcoholic.

Glenn's books were on the table where he left them the night before; he took a silent step in that direction.

"*What ee-vil lurks . . . in the hearts of man?*" his father's voice intoned, rising melodramatically from the kitchen floor.

His face presented a drunken smile and reddened eyes. "Trying to slip out on me," he said.

"Don't want to be late for school."

"C'mon—don't bullshit old bullshitter. May be stupid is true but weren't born yesterday." He seemed to wink.

Life with a drunk.

"I have a test at school—have to read my notes—have to hurry." Glenn opened the refrigerator door and not spotting anything to grab and eat, opened the bread box and removed a slice of bread from a package, knowing all along that his father was studying him with drunken scrutiny. Rolling the slice into a hot dog shape, Glenn took a bite, glanced his father's way.

"Today's the day—gonna dance with the angels," his father managed to say. "Today's the day—gonna slip across the great divide. Gonna see what it's all about on the other side—if you know what I mean."

"Know what you mean—know what you mean; think I've heard that before."

"Methinks someone has gotten up on the wrong side of the fucking bed."

"How you doing it this time?" Glenn said. He chewed even as his urge was to spit out the bread, to either run or cry.

"Son, don't mock me—don't do that."

"Asked a simple question. How you gonna do it? Got a new way to do it this time?"

One eye closed, a mean smile taking shape, his father tried to focus on him. A muscular working man, he was never predictable. "Wanted to, knock you flat on your ass," he said.

It was that tone Glenn had rarely heard. His father may never have hit him, but neither had he mocked his father in the midst of one of his threats to do away with himself. He stared back at the man, at his tone of voice, as if unafraid, took another bite of rolled bread. The creature who was his father stared back in turn.

Sickened, nerve and appetite gone all at once, Glenn removed the gob of bread from his mouth, tossed it in the wastebasket. His father might break something, in ferocious reaction, to make a point. He might, for dramatic effect, make a line of blood on his forearm with a paring knife. He had done all these, several of them together at times, had shattered whiskey bottles, coffee cups, plates of food against wall or floor. Once he snapped the blade of a butcher knife under his foot before cutting the back of his hand as if drawing a line with an ink pen, and another time, in another apartment, to make credible a philosophical point, gripped the refrigerator and tipped it to its side on the floor, showing an intoxicated grin which, the following Saturday, had them carrying boxes to the car and moving in silence to still another small apartment.

"Why don't you go to bed," Glenn said to the rheumy-eyed man.

"Why don't *you* go to bed?" his father said. "Why don't you kiss my ass."

"I would—I have to go to school."

"Can't give your dad the time of day here in his hour of need? Hey, wise guy?"

"Have to go to school."

"School? You have to go to school? What the hell is school? What the hell's anything, you can't learn to give one minute, to the one person, who happens to love you—in his hour of desperate need?" A mischievous line in his father's lips revealed that some of this was drunken acting. "Son, you know you're the only person, whole wide world, I ever really loved. Know that? It's true. Today, son. Know what today is? Day your old dad's waxing cross the *Rio Grande*—gonna see what it's like on the other *side-ay*."

"Have a nice time," Glenn said to the weaving, whiskered man. "Have a nice trip."

"Awh, son, don't make fun of me."

"Have to go to school—what do you expect me to do?"

"That all you can say?"

"How? That's what I asked in the first place. How you gonna do it this time?"

"Fact," his father said at last, as he swiveled his head around, got it into place to focus on him again. "Fact—you wanna know—I'll tell ya, goddammit. Gonna lay down here on a chair by the stove, gonna see how far I can travel on a dollar's worth of regular. Gonna put my weary head, my weary heart at rest at last. Son, tell me something. You believe in the Almighty?"

Glenn decided to give escape a try, stepped toward the door. "Won't the gas still be on? After you're gone on your trip?"

"Son, can't you give me an ounce of sympathy? Little drop a love's all I ask. 'At's all. You know, I'm so weary, so broken-spirited. I'm so defeated, I don't know what to do anymore. Simple goddam truth."

His father's words almost got to him, as they sometimes did. "Stop drinking," Glenn said. "Try that."

"I'm on the edge of the world looking down—that's what you say?"

Glenn remained within the moist focus of his father's eyes. For an instant Glenn feared he was going to break, in the face of which he said, "Don't know what else to say—have to go to school."

"Don't love your old dad—just a little?" the man asked with a faint smile.

"Not when he's like this, no, I don't—I don't love you anymore." Glenn managed not to break as he said this. "I hate it when you're like this you want to know the truth," he added. Don't break, he was telling himself. Keep your eyes on his.

"You know I'm just a drunken fool," his father said. "It's all over for me. I know it is, and you know it is. Son, I don't know what to do with myself. I just—need to know—that you love me. A little. One drop of love. I need something to take with me. All I'm asking. Little ticket into the kingdom of heaven. You need a ticket to get in, you see, or they won't let you dance with the angels. You know that? Ain't nobody else in this world can help me—except you. And if you can't dance with the—"

"Gotta go."

"You're my only ticket, son. You're all I have left in the world that counts for anything."

"Gotta go—I'm gonna be late for school."

"That's what you say? You're gonna be late for school? My life's on the line you say you're gonna be late for school?"

"What do you expect me to say? I don't know what to say anymore. All I know is I can't take this. I just can't take it anymore."

Another sly grin began to form on his father's face. "Say good-bye," he said. "That's all I'm asking you to do. Say good-bye. Say: Fare thee well, fare thee well old father in your forthcoming journey. Say: We'll meet again. Say: I love you as my old dad and we'll meet again. That's all I want to hear. Don't know where, don't know when. Who loves you—it's only ticket'll get you a single dance with the angels. Say: I love you as my old dad and we'll meet again. Say that for me."

"See you later. I'm gonna be late."

"Son—wait. Wait. I have to get on with this. Already out of my hands—know what I mean? I'm a little pie-eyed, I know. Mind's clear, though. Heart's certain. This old world—can't get along anymore, it's time for me to get on my way. Can't do it like I used to. Can't. Old world's got me by the balls, son, if you know what I mean."

"Might help," Glenn said to his father, "if you stopped saying 'know what I mean.' "

"Oh, son, jesus, your dad's an old dog with his tail between his legs. He'll do whatever you say. He needs your love. Just one word from his one and only pal of all time will get him over to the other side, will get him through the big door and dancing with the angels into eternity. Son, I just have to get out of here. It's what I have to do. Have to. Can't stay around anymore."

"Well—you do what you have to do," Glenn said with an edge which may have been either anger or hurt. "Let me tell you what I have to do. I come home after school. I come in the door, I'm going to have a cigarette burning. That way I won't have to look at you with your head in the stupid goddam oven—'cause everything will go BOOM and blow all to hell before I even see you. That's what I have to do. So you go ahead. Fill the place with gas. I don't care. Wherever you're going, I'll catch up with you. 'Cause I don't care anymore either. *Know what I mean?* You're crossing the great divide, then I'll be crossing, too—and we'll meet on the other side."

A new smile started into his father's face, in concert with his glossy eyes. Glenn knew at once that it was his own accidental rhyme, his own rhetorical flourish and the sentiment of melodrama and anger his father had been trying to draw from him all along. A gurgle of laughter and tears came from his father as he tried to contain himself, as he said, ". . . thought . . . tough guy . . . you didn't smoke."

Nor could Glenn stop his own face from reacting, as his eyes filmed over and something like laughter escaped his throat—even as he looked aside, not to be seen.

"See what heart you got," his father said softly. "Fulla heart. Know you are. Act tough as you want—you don't fool me."

Full of heart? Was it true that he was full of heart? Glenn wonders as he glances to the side again at Danny.

He loved his father, he knows that, but he doesn't know why he loved him. How could he come out of the mess that was their life together and love a man who was such a disaster, who made their life so miserable and worrisome, who caused so much hurt and unhappiness? Merely because he was his father? Was that all it was?

Should he hate him? he wonders. How is it that he has met so many sons who express only contempt for their own upstanding fathers? Was it time to reconsider? Had he loved his father—or was it something else? Had he been impaired long ago and not known it?

He recalls, too: Coming home after school, seeing his father's car where it should not have been so shocked him that for a moment he seemed unable to breathe. The car should have been in the parking lot near Buick Plant Three and his father should have been at work within the vast rumbling factory. However drunk or hungover, he always went to work. Had he kept his promise? Was his body in the kitchen, his head in the stove?

Glenn walked past the car, turned along the driveway between houses. His legs lost some strength and began to tremble as they had not trembled before. Should he do something? Should he go for help?

He had no cigarette in any case and only later would remember his promise to enter with one burning. The door was unlocked. No music was playing—the kitchen was empty. The remains of drinking were on table and counter. And—odd disappointment—the kitchen stove stood unused and unattended.

"Pop?" he said into the silent space.

He stepped to the swinging door, pushed it to let himself into the living room.

There was his father, slumped to his side on the old couch. Alive. His eyes were open, part of a curious smile. He was dressed in white shirt and tie, was alive. But as he saw his father's drunken smile he also saw that his sleeve near his left shoulder was glistening red and knew at once that it was blood. In the same glance he also saw a small wooden-handled pistol—it looked like a toy—on the floor near his father's shoes.

"*What happened?*" he uttered to the man slumped there.

His father kept looking at him; the line of his smile continued. "Accident."

"Accident? What are you saying? What accident?" However red-faced, however drunk it seemed he should be, his father seemed oddly sober.

"What I said. Little accident."

The faint smile continued. If Glenn believed him at all, he stopped believing him. It wasn't an accident. There was a gun. There was blood. Changed from his factory clothes of that morning he wore white shirt and tie. The tie was askew, as red as his face. He had shot himself. He had shot himself and he was bleeding. The old Navajo blanket was pulled down behind him, and other blood marks were on his suit pants, as if he had touched the blood and moved his hand and fingers around. Everything was a mess and something like a siren was circling in Glenn's mind. The old question: Oh God—what to do?

Maybe it was his father's smile that kept returning Glenn's reaction to anger. "How can you say accident?" he said. "Are you all right?"

"What I said. Little accident."

The faint smirk continued. Blood was under his arm, too, Glenn noticed. Glistening dark purple-red blood there under his arm. He was a mess. "Shit," Glenn said.

And he said, "Jesuschrist! Jesuschrist Almighty! What are you talking about? Goddam you! What are you talking about? Goddam you! You sonofabitch you! You were going to be here for me to find! An accident! How can you say that? HOW CAN YOU SAY THAT? GODDAM YOU! HOW CAN YOU SAY THAT SHIT?"

Glenn had started to cry, too, and his father's sly smirk was disappearing.

"I just want to go to school," Glenn cried out. "That's all I want to do. I just want to go to school like everybody else. How can you do this crap?"

His father kept looking his way, looked lost.

"Why don't you shoot *me?*" Glenn said. "Why don't you do that? I don't care! You think I care? Go ahead and do it. I don't care. I don't have any friends. Did you know that? It's true. I don't have any friends. Not at school or anywhere. It's because my old man's a stupid drunk. Did you know that? It's because my old man's a stupid fucking drunk. I know you know that, because it's true. Goddam you—you sonofabitch!"

His father's eyes were filling and Glenn looked to the floor not to see into them.

As Glenn wiped his eyes, tried to clear his vision and cry less, he only cried more.

He took breaths, swallowed, kept wiping his eyes, which kept putting forth tears he could not contain. He tried again to look at his father, and saw him staring aside with his own glossy eyes. "I'm going to call a doctor," Glenn said. "An ambulance."

His father looked back. "No, can't do that. No—it's just a flesh wound. All it is. Main thing, son, tell you the truth. Main thing—I'm having a hell of a time reaching my old jug there." Some of his sly smile was trying to make a comeback. "Tell you this," he said. "Good to see you even though you stab me right in the heart with what you say. Oh, son, goddam jesuschrist, welcome to hard times. Pour me a little something in a glass there, will you? Will you do that for me? I don't have any strength in this arm—and this one doesn't want to do a goddam thing either."

"You're just drunk—that's all you are. I feel sorry for you and all you are is drunk."

He did not pour his father a drink, although he was tempted to do so. Nor did he throw the bottle against the wall, even as such a smash occurred to him. However uncertainly, stepping to the table in the adjacent kitchen, taking the bottle by its neck, he stood at the sink and let the odorous booze splash down over the drain. "Throwing this shit away," he said.

"Hey, son, Glenn—jesus, don't do that! That's a waste of good money—son, don't do that!"

Glenn stopped. He turned the bottle upright in the sink as if he had emptied it all, although three or four inches remained. He kept his back to his father, expecting any moment to be swung around, to have the bottle grabbed.

As he looked back, though, his father was in the same position on the couch, watching him. His head was hanging some and he looked defeated all over again. The lost booze, it seemed, did not matter so much after all.

"Goddam, I'm sorry," the slumped man said. "I'm so goddam sorry. Don't blame you for being mad at me. Don't blame you for pouring away my booze. That's the problem, son. Can't do anything anymore. What I been trying to tell you. Goddam jug has me by the throat. Does. Messing up your life too. I know it is. That's why it kills me. It does, swear to God, because I know it's messing up your life too."

Glenn looked down at the top of his father's head, at his hair, where it was thinning. As uncertainly as he had poured the whiskey away, he said, "There's some left."

His father's face changed; he couldn't help smiling through his tears. "Thank God for small favors," he said. "Thought my ship was sunk there, I'll tell you. Pour me a little in a glass, will you? Arm's so weak don't think I can do anything right now."

At the sink, Glenn poured a slug into a drinking glass. As he stepped back and handed it to his father, placed it in the fingers of his right hand, he said, "Is it bleeding—it looks like it is."

"Guess it is. Ah, son, it's all been beating me down. Would you give me a cigarette there? A light? Can't do anything anymore."

Taking up the Pall Malls and Zippo, Glenn put them in his father's hands.

"Tell you, you were here earlier I think we coulda beat 'em off. Coming at me from all sides, by land and by sea, if you know what I mean. Oops—goddam, not supposed to say that. Had a hell of a time anyway just staying on my feet, I'll tell you that."

"Yeah, well no more drunk talk," Glenn heard himself say. "No more drunk talk. I'm sick of it."

"Well," his father said. And added, smiling, "Okay. I guess you're the boss. Okay."

"Don't make fun of me either," Glenn said to his father.

His father made a face, as if to say okay, he'd go along. "I guess I am bleeding a little," he said.

There was the pistol, still on the floor. As he moved closer, Glenn used the toe of his right shoe to nudge the pistol out of sight under the couch, thinking that if he stepped on it, it might go off.

He lifted his father's left arm at the wrist, and at the elbow, too, to see what he could see. There, closer, were the warm boozy smells of his father as he had always known them. There too was the watery blood.

That part of his father's shirt was soaked red. Replacing his left hand in his lap, Glenn unbuttoned the white shirt beginning at the belly. "I'm going to take this off," he said. "The tie too."

His father, to his surprise, sat under his hands like an obedient patient. Glenn loosened the necktie, pulled the slighter end from the knot. His father cooperated, turned his left hand as Glenn unbuttoned the cuff, leaned forward a little as he pulled the shirttails from his pants. It was then, a greater surprise, that Glenn noticed a small rip in the shirt cloth near his father's underarm, to the side of his breast, around which there was the thickest amount of glistening blood.

"Hold still a second," Glenn said. Going to the kitchen, he returned with two dish towels from a drawer and a grocery bag from where they stuffed them in beside the refrigerator.

Putting the whiskey glass aside, Glenn removed the shirt over his father's right hand, gathered it behind his back and around to his left side. The shirt, being removed, was releasing a new musty pickle odor from his father. Glenn eased the shirt down over his shoulder, wadding the bloody part inside, folded and wadded it toward his father's left hand—which still held his Zippo and package of cigarettes—where it rested in his lap.

"What's with this hand?" Glenn said. "This arm?"

His father looked to him from fifteen inches or so. There were his red floating eyes, the skin around them loose, and there was his stubble and full lips. "Just wants to stay there," he said. "Doesn't want to go anywhere."

"You can't move it?"

"Not too well right now, doc, but I guess I can."

His father gave effort on that side, lifted his arm some as Glenn wadded the shirt some more and pulled it over his hand, leaving him in his less bloody sleeveless undershirt. "Maybe you hit a tendon or something?" Glenn said, stuffing the wadded shirt into the grocery bag.

"Don't think so. Flesh is all."

There was the wound itself. Above his breast, to the side of the strap of the undershirt, a tear in his flesh disappeared under his arm. Glenn leaned in closer to look. Rather than a hole it looked like an open valley of meat. As he looked, a bubble of blood grew on the lower nipple side of the valley and broke over the edge.

The blood escaping looked thin, like red water. A leaky faucet. He raised his father's arm some in both hands, to see under his arm to where the valley ended. His underarm was marked, too, beyond the tear, braised enough to bleed, but not like the torn flesh. Maybe two and a half inches long, the tear looked to be half an inch wide and almost as deep.

"Didn't go in your arm," Glenn said. He lifted his father's arm all the more, to see if there were any other rips in his flesh, under his arm. "Must be in the couch—or in the wall. The bullet. Does it hurt?"

"Just when I try to lift, like this," his father said, using his chin to indicate his left side. "Guess it jarred my ribs."

"Looks like it should be sewn up."

"Well—can't do that," his father said. "Some doc sees it's a gunshot I think he'd have to report it. Just can't do that. Couldn't afford that."

"Undershirt's coming off, too," Glenn said to the odorous man. "Can't afford what?"

"Don't know and don't wanna find out," his father said. "Way my luck's been going they'd probably fine me and put me in jail, fire me from my job, take away my medical insurance and stick you in reform school as a wayward child, for good measure."

Glenn finished removing the sleeveless undershirt, getting it over one arm, and down over the wounded side. Wadding it, folding it into itself, he used it to daub at and wipe his father's side, and stuffed it into the bag with the wadded white dress shirt. Like water surfacing, the wound put forth another fresh red flow over the edge. Blood had dried in layers; some was dry and some, under the new flow, was still sticky and gave off the musty odor.

"What a mess," Glenn said. He took one of the dish towels to the kitchen sink, to soak it with water. "What a lousy shot," he added, even as despair was in him again.

"Don't make me laugh—hurts too much."

Nothing was funny to Glenn. Anger festered up and down in him as he used the cloth to wipe his father's chest and side, and under his arm, working around the ripped flesh.

"You wanted me to come home and find you croaked," Glenn said. At last his father said, "I didn't want that."

"Yeah, tell me about it."

Glenn continued to wipe sticky blood from his father's side and ribs. Another fullness slipped from the wound, and his father said, "Pour me another little snort there, will you?"

"Screw you," Glenn said. He wiped some more. "Things get hot for you, you want a drink. You think I'd get a charge out of coming home and finding your dead body? Screw you."

His father let a moment pass. Then he said, not kindly, "Don't get too tough now."

His father's authority only irritated Glenn now. "I'm going to wash this out," he said. "I'm going to pour in some Mercurochrome. And tape it up. If it doesn't stop bleeding, I'm going to call a doctor. That's what I'm going to do. I don't care what you say and I'll get as tough as I want. So screw you, old man."

"Told you we can't call any doctors—it's what I mean."

"Or I might take you to an emergency room. What're you going to do—say you'll knock me on my ass?"

"You're gonna have to be the doc here," his father said, as if Glenn had not spoken at all. "We're gonna have to rough it out. Got no choice. You can't help, I'll go it on my own. No cops, no insurance agents, no big shots from Buick Motor Company. Iwo Jima, son, that's what it is. Normandy Invasion. Inchon Reservoir. Your old dad has taken a flesh wound and you're the medic here and soon's you patch him up, he'll be good as new. Almost good as new. Sonofabitch does hurt some, I'll tell you that. Hurts above my elbow, like the bones got jarred or something. Now give me a goddam drink. You may be tough and may think you're going to take over—but give me a goddam drink before you do anything rash."

Glenn's defiance stiffened—the last thing he'd do was get his father a drink—and using a wet end of the dish towel, he jabbed directly upon the wound.

"Ahh!" His father flinched.

"Don't be a crybaby," Glenn said. "We're on the beach at Normandy—don't have time for crybabies. Moving out at oh-four-hundred. Jerries have a machine gun nest and we're going to knock it out."

His father could not help snickering, trying—against the pain it caused—not to laugh.

Glenn looked close again upon the wound. The gash, the bottom of which was difficult to actually see, continued to fill with blood. "Keeps bleeding," he said. Again, his anger had lifted.

"You'd make a pretty good doc," his father said. "You know that?"

Returning from the bathroom with the bottle of Mercurochrome, studying the wound where it continued to produce blood, Glenn daubed it with the towel. "Hope I don't have to amputate," he said.

His father tittered some more.

"May sting," Glenn said. "I sure as hell hope so." He poured perhaps half of a teaspoon of orange-black Mercurochrome into and over the wound. At once, as it ran over his father's side like ink, Glenn wiped and pressed to check the rivulets. There was no flinching, and he said, "I'm just sorry we don't have some iodine."

His father smiled some more. "Tell you it hurts to laugh," he said.

"Okay," Glenn said, to himself as much as to his father. "What I'm going to do—I'm going to get some tape, and I'm going to do that again, with the Mercurochrome. Then I'm going to cover it and tape it. Then—you're going to bed. If it doesn't stop bleeding—I'm going to call a doctor. Or I'm going to get you to an emergency room and you can say you fell on something."

His father, listening, watching, smiled at him.

"I'm serious," Glenn said. "It's what we're going to do so don't give me any crap about anything or I'll knock you even flatter on your ass than you already are."

"Aye, aye," his father said. "You're the captain."

Flooding the wound again, Glenn used a knife to cut a section of clean dish towel. Finding but three or four inches of old adhesive tape on a metal spool in the bathroom, he used a roll of sticky black friction tape from the tool box under the sink. Crossing long segments of tape in an X pattern, he tried, even as his father squirmed in pain, to pull the sides of flesh together, to cut off the bleeding. For good measure, he crossed the X with a couple others, to pull the wound together from several directions.

"That might stop the bleeding," he said as he studied the double-X's of black tape as closely as a doctor. "But I don't know if it'll heal if it's not stitched or something."

"Son, listen, Monday I'll take it to the shop nurse and say it was something on the job. I need a shot, she can give me a shot. I'm right there at work, nurse won't think it happened somewhere else, although I'll have to get this black tape cleaned off by then."

"It doesn't seem to be bleeding now."

"I think you did a good job."

"Okay—into bed," Glenn said, straightening up.

"Son, give me a little snort there, will you?"

"Maybe in a minute," he said. "I don't know. Right now—you get to bed."

"Goddam, admiral, don't overdo it. Gotta take a leak."

Glenn took in his father's sour booze and tobacco odor as he helped guide him to the bathroom. There, as his father said, "I'll just sit down for a bit," Glenn helped lower him to the stool.

"You're on your own," he told him.

Moments later, helping his father to his bedroom, to a seat on the side of his bed, Glenn looked closely at the taped dressing to see if it was bleeding around the edges. The white folds of towel showed red in the middle, but not so much that the wound seemed to be putting forth blood as it had before. He removed his father's shoes and socks, pulled his pants over his feet. "You're a mess," he said.

"Doc, how about some aspirin and a little drink, whatta ya say?"

In a moment, returning with three aspirin in the cap and an inch of whiskey in the glass, Glenn placed them one at a time in his father's right hand. His father sipped until the glass was empty and placed it on the night table close by. "You're a good ole doc," he said. "Tell you that."

"Yeah, sure."

"I mean it. You're one of those guys can do about anything he wants, that's what you are. Redsie, I'm gonna tell you something important. Don't think 'cause I messed up my life you can't do something with yours. You got a real head on your shoulders. That's no bullshit either, I'm tellin' ya the truth."

Looking at him still, his father was growing teary-eyed. "Doctor was what you wanted to be, you know, or anything else," he said. "Don't ever think you couldn't do it. It can be done, you're the guy can do it. It's one of the reasons I love you like I do."

He positioned his father on the bed on his good side, lifting the sheet and blanket to his shoulder.

"Tell you something else, partner," his teary-eyed father said. "You ever want to take a run at something like that, you know, it would be an honor, would be my honor—I'd do anything in the world to help you. Any kind of work. Any hours. I'd have something to live for, you know. I'd work like a dog. There's nothing I wouldn't do for you and I mean that with all my heart."

Even as he smiled, his father's eyes remained full. Drunk, Glenn thought. Drunk again.

"Wanna know something else?" his father said.

He looked at him.

"The goddamned thing just went off on me. Was an accident."

Glenn could not help smiling a little. His father's eyes filled all the more. "You had it in mind, though," is all Glenn said to him. He knew it wasn't an accident.

"Who doesn't have it in mind?" his father said. "Thing is—might not hold up in court—was an accident. Redsie—I want you to know something. You're about all I have to live for—goddam truth is I don't deserve you."

Drunk talk, Glenn thought. And accident or not, he knew too that someday his father was going to succeed. He would go off and leave him, and would leave behind the message Glenn did not want to hear, that it wasn't drunk talk at all.

Danny brings him back. They are in the large parking lot before the Biddeford Arena and he is handing Danny his gear from the back of the station wagon. Bag, sticks, team jersey on a hanger. "Alan said Coach Busch is going to kick him off the team if he doesn't pay," Danny says.

Glenn needs a second to take in that Danny is talking about his friend Alan Lebrie. "Alan told you that?" he says.

"It's what he said."

"He hasn't told his parents?"

"I don't think he has."

"You heard the Coach say that—that he was going to kick him off the team?"

"No. But I heard him ask when he was going to pay. Everyone did. Alan told me his parents can't pay it anyway so it didn't matter."

"Slow down now. Of course it matters. Did you hear Mister Busch say he was going to kick him off the team?"

"No."

The two-hundred-dollar fee is more than Glenn can afford and he says, "Well, Coach Busch knows for sure that Mister Frankenthaler would pay Alan's fee. I'm sure he paid it last year. When did Alan tell you this?" As he lifts the tailgate, Glenn sees the subject of their conversation, Alan Lebrie, standing at the end of their row of cars, also draped in equipment, waiting for Danny to catch up for the walk into the arena.

"After practice outdoors. Why don't they have any money?"

"Well, I'll tell you sometime. There's Alan right now—he's waiting for you."

"They have a car," Danny says, glancing around to spot his friend. He waves; Glenn waves too.

"It's an old car. Listen—tell Alan not to worry. He's not going to be kicked off the team. I'm sure Mister Frankenthaler will pay his fee—but don't say that to him. If there's any problem I'll cook up something with the other parents and take care of it."

"You will?"

"I will. Go ahead now. Be careful—good luck in your game."

Under his load, only a step away as Glenn is turning to use his key on the Wagoneer's rear electric window, Danny says, "Alan doesn't have money for pizza either."

Glenn smiles. Their pattern after Biddeford games—a near tradition by now—is to drive to a nearby pizza parlor for a midday meal, a part of the trip many of them enjoy more than the game itself. "Tell him not to worry about that either," Glenn says. "I'll take care of the pizza."

"Thanks, Dad," Danny says, smiling—he alone of his two children thanks him when he is pleased—as he turns to catch up with his friend, probably to tell him the good news about the pizza.

There, too, are Alan's parents, moving together at the father's slow gait. They are beyond the parking lot on their way to the row of doors across the front of the arena. The slight man moves his right leg and foot, then pauses to lift the left the same distance. Glenn also notices their car, a dull and dented sixties clunker with a peeling landau roof. The car, he knows, is neither registered nor inspected and he guesses they start it up only on mornings like these, when they can slip unnoticed from New Hampshire into the adjacent state of Maine.

Pleased in any case to please his younger son—the genuineness of whose thank you's always warms him—he finishes closing the tailgate. Rather than go along to the arena right now, however, he slips back in behind the wheel and closes the door. Something is unfolding in him still and unsure yet what it is, he wants some more moments alone.

Mist has already clouded the windows and he welcomes the dim concealment within the car. He'll just sit for a couple minutes, he thinks. Usually he doesn't make it across the parking lot before another parent joins him and starts a story or joke, or begins putting forth an opinion on some issue at the university where most of them are employed.

Alan Lebrie and the coach, Phil Busch, are on his mind. So is his father lingering about the fringes of things. Or at the heart of things. Yes, at the heart of things, he thinks, as he realizes he is within that grip, that emotion, which seems to take over when he thinks of his father. Is this part of the inheritance, he wonders, left to him by his father's tipping all those bottles? Will music always play like this when it isn't playing at all?

Peter Frankenthaler, a man Glenn's age who loves to trade jokes, is standing with a gathering of other parents at the Coffee Counter inside the entrance to the cavernous arena. Glenn waits for a punch line to be delivered—by Dave Kreisler, whose son is the star scorer and who is always telling funny stories of his kosher upbringing in Brooklyn—before he says, aside, "Peter, can I talk to you for a minute?"

Their local philanthropist, Peter has to know that such an opening is going to cost him money, Glenn thinks. If he has ever felt objections, though—picking up tabs for more uniforms, equipment, band instruments, entry fees and travel expenses than the town itself—he has kept them to himself. They walk to a further bank of entrance doors, where Glenn says, "It's Alan Lebrie. He told Danny he thinks Phil is going to kick him off the team because he still hasn't paid his registration fee."

"I was afraid of that," Peter says, making it clear he knows all about the problem. "That Alan—he's more of an old Granite Stater than Phil Busch. I'll take care of it. Thanks for letting me know. Thank Danny."

As Peter Frankenthaler heads away, under the bleachers in the direction of the locker rooms at the other end of the arena, Glenn hesitates, then wanders along that way himself. He has no feeling this morning, he realizes, to hear stories about Brooklyn. A loner. Standoffish. The old charges. The truth is, he thinks, he is in a mood too oddly emotional to enter into conversation with anyone, unless it is Danny.

At the far end, turning away from the doors to the locker rooms, he slips into a seat behind the Plexiglas and goalie's net where he knows he is likely to remain alone. When the game starts, he can stand near the glass and see the action in that end close up, even if action at the other end will be almost out of view.

A few minutes later their team of eleven- and twelve-year-old sons comes skating through an opened gate onto the ice, joined almost at once by the sons of the other team. He looks as always for Danny, spots his fluid movement in blue and white, the certain way he carries himself, before ascertaining from his number, 4, and his name, too, across his shoulders, WHALEN, that it is he. As always, too, the sight of Danny moving as he does makes him smile with pleasure. Danny is not, like his older brother, a ferocious all-star player in these Pee Wee games; nor does his brother, or anyone else, have Danny's magically fluid skating skills, his speed and quickness.

Thinking he sees Danny glance to the bleachers at mid-ice where he usually sits with the other parents, Glenn stands up next to the Plexiglas, to catch his eye when he comes around again. It is like Danny to check in with his father, if only visually, while his brother, in some scheme of intense game preparation, only looked to exchange glances in the game itself, when he scored or assisted well, or received a penalty, all of which occurred frequently, to signal to his father whatever it was that such a brief glance, and a tip of his stick, too, might signal. Either sign, from either son, always pleased him. Sometimes he gave a small sign in turn, a move of his hand, a nod. Or he might wink, for the good feeling it gave him, even as he knew his winks could not be seen at that distance.

Gliding around, Danny spots him and puts up a rainbow of fine ice as he skates over and turns to an instantaneous stop. Danny's feet seem so light, so certain and natural in their movements, Glenn cannot help thinking that he might as easily be a figure skater, although it is not something he is inclined to mention to his son in their town of so many ice ponds and hockey teams.

"Hey, Pa!" Danny says on a smile between panels of Plexiglas, as if he had not just seen his father half an hour ago.

"Go get 'em, have a good game," Glenn says, smiling happily in turn. Danny calls him Pa, he has noticed, when he is in an especially good mood.

As quickly, Danny is gone, skimming over the ice toward the other end, where his teammates are circling to start their warm-up drills. Glenn remains standing, to watch, and something of the wonder of the moment flashes through him. They played Purely Pickups on the drive over and now they are here, and this is how they live. Blessings counted; all is well. Someday, he imagines, he will look back on these hours and want to have them back. Purely Pickups with Danny as a twelve-year-old on a Saturday morning in the winter long ago. A few words passed between panels of Plexiglas. Love each step of the way, he knows, even as he knows too that it cannot last and may be taken from him. But whoever had sense enough to arrest time, even if they could?

In the moment of removing the pistol from under the couch, a half-formed thought of shooting himself passed through his mind. He did not shoot himself, to be sure, but the thought was there like a butterfly landing, fluttering up, landing again.

He continued cleaning up—found the hole in the Navajo blanket— and the butterfly landed, fluttered again. The sensation was sweet, intoxicating, tempting.

Leaving the apartment, he carried the grocery bag of bloody clothes in one hand and the pistol in his jacket pocket in the other. Stuffing the bag into a garbage can next to the alley where they lived, he walked on with the pistol in his hand inside his jacket pocket. His thought was to get rid of it—he had no idea where or how—so it couldn't be used again.

He stopped—the moments still occur in dreams—on the "singing" bridge surrounded by Buick factories. The pedestrian walkway was contained in a trellis of bolted metal, the river flowing by below. The skyline of downtown was close to the factories and standing there with a pistol in his hand in his pocket was like something from movies he had seen and paperbacks he had read, but the melodrama did not transport him, he could tell, as he was always wanting to be transported.

He slipped the pistol from his jacket, held it over the railing. To passing cars, he thought, he must look like someone pausing to gaze upon water and skyline; the railing concealed what was in his hand. He wondered at the time how anyone could want to die like that. To end his life. To miss everything. The butterfly fluttered and another rush, another desire raced in his heart.

He aimed the pistol at the water. As cars passed nearby, neither moving nor bracing himself in any way, he squeezed the trigger. *Pfft!* The kick was slight; his hand barely jumped. Nor was the sound noticeable against the tires' songs and the V-8's and straight sixes being stamped and welded and assembled all along the river.

"Watch it, little fishes," he said aloud. *Pfft! Pfft!* Five shots altogether. He fired into the dark water until the gun would fire no more. He squeezed harder, to be sure the gun was empty, in fear that it would be fished out of the river and used accidentally.

In a momentary absence of headlights flickering through the grillwork of the bridge he side-armed the small weight of wood and metal out over the water. There came a splash in the darkness, thirty-odd feet away.

He stood there. Not relief, but fear came up in him. Death and life were so close, the small gun had said to him.

An urge rose in him to go home, and it was something else he would not quite forget. Most of the time what he thought of as home was a small set of empty rooms, but this night someone was there. Maybe his father would be asleep, maybe he would remain asleep throughout the evening and night, but he was there and the rooms would not be empty. The man who loved him. Life with an alcoholic. But love attracted, it did not repel.

The game has ended. The horn has blared and brought Glenn back again—lines of boys are passing, slapping hands as they glide to the gate to leave the ice. The clock overhead is going dark as he looks up, and he misses seeing the score. He sits a few more minutes before getting to his feet to make his way along the stands. He has never sat through a game without knowing who won and he tries—however aware he remains that something is still unfolding in him—to find the predicament amusing. He won't tell anyone. He'll figure it out from what is said.

Other parents are gathering near the doors, waiting as always for their pizza-minded sons to remove gear and skates, to come lugging bags, sticks, jerseys. There, as it suddenly happens, are Mr. and Mrs. Lebrie, he with his one-sided frail stance, she with her excessive lipstick, and Glenn says at once, before he can think about it, moving in close with a smile, "Pizza is my treat today and I don't want to hear one word about it."

A pause begins; he has caught them off guard. It could go either way.

A smile begins to form on the face of Galen Lebrie. "You insist," he says. "Won't hear me say a word." Grace Lebrie smiles, too, beside her husband.

Glenn is pleased. He did it. "Kids played a good game," he says. "Alan always goes all out, doesn't he?"

"Just loves it," Grace Lebrie says. "Alan just lives for these games."

"Well so do we, don't we?" Galen Lebrie adds. "Wouldn't be fair not to admit that. Don't know what we'll do when Alan gets too old to play."

No one speaks for a moment but they stand together as friends. Red Whalen at work, Glenn thinks. He imagines his father looking down on him, pleased. Not flashy like your old man, he imagines him saying. But you're coming along.

Loading Danny's gear into the car, having him in the front seat beside him for the drive to the pizza parlor, it comes to Glenn again how much he enjoys these outings with his younger son. A number of parents in their town refuse to "chauffeur" their children, others object to teams of any kind or just to hockey. A friend, a sculptor, smiled as he remarked to Glenn, "You working-class types, you live through your children." It is and is not true, Glenn believes, reluctant to admit how bothered he was by the remark. At the same time he has wondered all along if the parents who come up with so many objections are not missing more than they know.

"We win?" Danny says beside him.

Glenn needs a moment to understand what Danny is asking. "You know something," Glenn says. "I don't know if you did or not."

Danny is taking a long side look at him. "You *don't?*" he says. It happens that Danny overlooks scores now and then, but his father always knows such things. Danny keeps smiling, increasingly pleased with this turn.

"Had my mind on other things," Glenn says.

"Pa doesn't know the score!" Danny says more or less to the ceiling and it may be the first time, it occurs to Glenn, that his younger son has felt bold enough to tease him. "Doesn't know the score!" Danny is thrilled—it has to be more of a thrill than the game—and they both continue to laugh as they drive along.

It is as he is at the counter, waiting to carry part of their order back to the table where Galen and Grace, Alan and Danny are seated, that Glenn begins to see what it is that has been working all day toward the front of his mind. Even as the teenage girl there places the drinks in paper cups on a tray and he smiles at her in turn, the life and death of past and present continue to come home to him.

Nor does a trembling within cease as he carries the tray to the table, where they joke and smile over heavy cups of Coke and ice, or as he carries the empty tray back to the counter for another load. He loved his father, he can see now, because he knew without any doubt that his father loved him. It was all so simple and what was more important at last than that? Forsaking vices, teaching Sunday school—they did not matter finally. Bringing home lots of money—it had to help but it did not matter either. Love alone was the only gift that survived.

The tray, balanced carefully, holds two of the three pizzas, and he and the girl behind the counter puzzle over the task of carrying the third while his thoughts continue in pursuit of life and death. Suicide will get into your blood, he can see, and here it is, making its way to the surface at last. The desire is there within him, he knows in his heart as he carries the pizzas to the table. The desire is there within him and it is a sweet desire, and it transports him now, lifts him, and all along he had lived with the illusion that his father had left him so little.

THE HEARING

T he weather on the morning of the hearing—a Saturday in April—
was disappointingly cold. The remains of soot- and sand-filled snow had
melted, there had been an occasional balmy afternoon, and grass here
and there was making its change from brown to green. The air this
morning, although sunny, was windy and cold, the temperature was
down to perhaps thirty degrees, and the previous days seemed a with-
drawn promise, a false spring.

Alex and his father drove through town to the courthouse well ahead
of their nine o'clock appointment. They were quiet and polite with each
other. In the building itself they waited in the corridor outside Mr.
Quinn's office. They stopped to sit on a bench there because his father
made a gesture that they sit down, and Alex made no mention of Mr.
Quinn's office waiting room. He felt ushered and silenced, however
much the day seemed to be his, by the authority of his father, of Mr.
Quinn, of the judge.

A sprawling black woman sat on the same bench, a thin, frog-eyed
boy beside her. Alex and his father sat knee to knee. Alex, stiff in his
white shirt and tie, his sports jacket and slacks, his polished shoes and
freshly combed hair, placed his awkward hands on his thighs. He was
still cold from not having worn a topcoat. At a bench directly opposite
was another woman, white, a factory badge from AC Spark Plug on her

purse strap. She was smoking a lipstick-marked cigarette; a thin, lipstick-marked teenage girl sat beside her.

His father—unlike himself, sober as he was—began to talk with the two mothers. He said, "I guess they'll learn something today, won't they?"

Almost in unison, the two women said, "I'll say," and "They surely will."

His father said, "I suppose we'll all learn a thing or two."

The women nodded and within a moment the three adults were talking of the cold weather, and bravely, strangers to their children, of life itself, agreeing with the notion that everyone made a few mistakes along the way. The black woman told a story that she had read, in *Reader's Digest*, she thought, of a mother somewhere, in Texas she thought, driving a truck to the prison to say good-bye to her son and then to drive his body home herself when he was hanged, or electrocuted, she wasn't sure which it was, but that poor mother waiting in her truck, she knew when her boy was going, she could feel it just like it was herself. Alex's father said, "That's why they got us here today," and the women looked off or down in silence.

When Mr. Quinn came out, Alex felt a mixture of pride and shame over the presentation of his father, pride for his appearance, his dress—factory worker or not, he carried his expensive hound's-tooth topcoat, and silk scarf, blood-colored, over the arm of his expensive suit—and shame for the exposure he felt as his father's son. He flushed then with embarrassment, for, as if still talking to the two women, his father responded to Mr. Quinn's introducing himself by saying, "We're all set if you are," offering to shake hands, reaching his hand out, holding it there as Mr. Quinn shifted a manilla folder to free his right hand, and shaking hands, Alex thought, as if he had met someone in a bar.

Alex walked behind the two men down the corridor, squeezed from a threesome. At the elevator door, they separated to let him enter first. Mr. Quinn ran things and they rose two or three floors in the silent box, and stepped into another corridor. Mr. Quinn gestured to the right with the manilla folder and Alex walked in the front this time. Mr. Quinn stopped at an oversized wooden door, which he opened gently, and when he glanced in, he stood to the side and held the door behind his arm. He nodded yes for them to enter. Alex walked in first, his father behind him. He paused just inside until his father was beside him. Mr. Quinn came around as if they had entered a church and ushered them with silent head motions to two ordinary armless wooden chairs in the center of the room. Alex felt a point of pressure in his bladder. He had to urinate now, but he was afraid to say so.

The judge had been reading and he had raised his eyes alone as if looking over glasses, although not wearing glasses. The Honorable Charles R. Flynn. He gave a slight nod. The greeting was so uncertain and the protocol of Juvenile Court so unknown that both Alex and his father ignored it. The judge kept his eyes on them as they sat down. When they were settled, seated at least, and Mr. Quinn was stepping to the side, the judge said, "Excuse me just one minute, please," and returned to reading some papers he held in his resting hands. Mr. Quinn took a seat to the side, fearlessly scraping the chair legs over the floor. Alex, feeling as if he had taken a seat on a stage, moved his knees closer together, to contain the pressure in his bladder. He held his head straight and did not look around.

He had expected the judge to sit at an elevated bench, and to wear black robes, as in the movies, but the man wore a dark suit and sat at a desk. There was a flag on a stand behind him, and ferns and broad-leafed plants on tables, and shelves, filled with dark-covered books. His desk, in the foreground, was as large as a small bed. The flag, glossy nylon, fringed with brass-colored strings, seemed an assurance that black robes or not, an authority was there that could impose punishment.

In time, in the silence, as the judge continued so slowly to read whatever it was he was reading, Alex looked down and stared at his hands in his lap. He tried to read their topography of veins and lines and hairs; within a moment he was only staring. His father had warned him that morning as they dressed that nothing would be funny or easy, and it was not. His father had also promised to be with him, to stick with him, but for the moment, if only a couple feet away, Alex felt he was out of reach. He thought of the white Oldsmobile, and felt a flash of panic, which he tried to conceal by not moving. Was there any way they could know about that white Oldsmobile?

He glanced to the side, at his father. As if they were schoolboys in the principal's office, Alex thought darkness might be made light on a secret smile. His father sat looking ahead. Alex knew his father had seen him on the periphery of his vision and for a moment he felt lost.

The judge began at last by explaining, in a monotone and not very clearly, that this was a hearing, but the court had the authority to impose sentence, and if they wanted they might be represented by counsel. He reviewed the charges against Alex, charges that did not recall a sense of the crimes but a sense of the time itself. The judge did not say Alex had stolen, he said he had "unlawfully driven away" fourteen automobiles. Looking at the papers before him, he mentioned the switched license plates, one car's spare tire Alex had traded for three dollars in gas, the Chevrolet sedan he had damaged in the amount of "three hundred nineteen dollars nineteen cents," an unforgettable figure, and a woman's coat from one car he had given to "Miss Eugenia Rodgers, aged fifteen, G-five-twenty-seven-forty-three Birch Road, Shiawassee Township, whose mother, Mrs. Jean Osborn, notified police . . ."

Alex sat all this time looking at his hands in his lap. He held his back straight and sat straight, not to present what had always been called defiance. There were hundreds of lines on his hands. They looked as fine as the far-off branchwork of winter trees. He felt the pressure mount again in his bladder.

The judge continued. He was talking now as well as reading, explaining that the spare tire had been recovered and returned to the owner, as had the coat, that the owner of the damaged Chevrolet in a signed statement to the county prosecutor had decided not to bring suit for damages that were covered by his insurance policy . . .

When the judge stopped talking, Alex looked up and saw that the man was looking at him. "Is this account complete?"

"Yes sir."

"Nothing withheld?"

"No sir." Awareness of the white Oldsmobile flashed through him.

"What do you have to say for yourself?"

Saying this, the judge looked down and began turning over some of the sheets again on his desk. But he was listening. In a moment, without looking up, he said, "Go on."

Alex had no planned alibi, but he had often imagined giving some credible explanation of himself. Now, as if out of breath, he said, "I don't know."

The judge turned his eyes up and looked directly at him for a moment, and looked down again. When he spoke now it was without looking up from the papers. "Why did you do these things?" he said.

Alex still did not know what to say. He said, "I'm not sure. Just to show off, I guess." He thought he would anger the judge but the man did not look up; he continued looking at the papers before him. In a moment, still looking down, he said, "Mr. Quinn, has your office anything to offer?"

Mr. Quinn stood up to speak and on his first remarks Alex looked back at his hands. "This is a simple pattern of divorced parents," Mr. Quinn said. "A lack of guidance and example in the home, and a drinking situation in the home."

Alex tried not to listen; he looked down at his hands again and made no attempt to glance at his father. He understood now what he did not quite understand before, that, as his father had warned him, it was not the crimes they were interested in, it was who they were.

Mr. Quinn went on speaking of "the mother," and "the brother," of his "driving most of the cars to Lake Nepinsing where the brother lived with the mother and her new husband," and of his "history in school," saying that he was "bright and adaptable," that he "has learned over the years to see to most of his needs, takes care of his own laundry, keeps his own room, fixes many of his own meals," and then of his "progress since his release from the detention home," that he was "up early now every morning to take care of a *Detroit Free Press* paper route . . ."

When the judge spoke, when Mr. Quinn had finished and stepped back to his chair, it was again without looking up. He said, as if to the papers on his desk, "Mr. Housman, what is your occupation?"

"I work over here at the Chevrolet, in Plant Four," his father said. His father's voice was diminished, slightly off key. Alex sat looking down again.

The judge said, "What type of work do you do, sir?"

"Die setter," his father said.

"How long have you been employed at Chevrolet?"

"Close to nineteen years."

"And before that?"

"Well, that doesn't count close to four years I spent in the army, and before that I worked for the railroad, back in Arkansas. But that's when I was a youngster, a young fella."

Alex sat looking down. It was not the language—*a youngster, a young fella*—which he had never heard his father use before, it was the telescoping of his father's life. Was this all? Was this what all the stories amounted to?

"Mr. Housman," the judge said. "Can you explain why your son has gotten into this trouble? This is quite serious, you know."

His father was slow in answering. After a moment he said, "I'm not entirely sure. Things have always been more or less hard on us—"

The judge interrupted. "Well, how do you feel about this?" he said. "Your son says he was showing off, now you say you're not entirely sure. That's not saying very much, is it? That is not why we are here today, I assure you. I'd like to know how you feel about this."

"That's a hard question," his father said. "I think they were awful foolish things to do. I hold myself more to blame than him. We have a family car, and we could have worked out a way for him to use it. I don't think he's done anyone near as much harm as he's done himself."

"Well, sir, there was damage in excess of three hundred dollars. There was untold inconvenience suffered. The law was broken. Just to mention a few things. Which do in fact cause harm to someone, do they not?"

"Yes, yes, they do. I just meant to say he's also harmed himself."

"I know what you meant to say, Mr. Housman," the judge said. He stared directly at Alex's father for a moment. Then he said, "What of this drinking situation?"

His father did not answer.

"I'd advise you to see to it," the judge said.

The judge began to write. Alex glanced at his father, who sat looking ahead. A ringlet of hair which had fallen to his father's forehead did not look rakish here as it did when he was drinking. Alex all at once pained in his heart for his father. The judge continued to write; he lifted a sheet, turned it over. Alex felt that he had to speak or he was going to wet himself. "Excuse me, please," he said. "I have to go to the lavatory."

The judge looked up but said nothing. Mr. Quinn said, "I'll take him, sir," and rose from his chair.

Alex did not look at his father. He followed Mr. Quinn across the room and through the door. In the corridor Mr. Quinn said, "It's right down here," and Alex followed.

"Nervous?" Mr. Quinn said.

"Yes."

"Wish I could tell you something, but I don't know what to say. I wouldn't worry too much, though."

Alex said nothing to this; Mr. Quinn said, "This is it right here. You go ahead. I'll wait out here for you."

Alex opened the door, which had MEN printed in peeling black on old frosted glass, and walked in. The room was clean, and there was an association of the detention home. He stepped up to one of the urinals. A window, to the side, was opened a slice, and the cold air was strong enough to smell. He imagined slipping through the window and running away and knew that it was only a foolish fantasy. He looked to the left, at the booth, but saw no shoes, no trouser folds, on the floor. He was alone in the room. At the sink he ran water on his hands. He dried them on rough paper towels. There he was before himself in the mirror; a new white shirt, sewed-in collar tabs not quite concealed, a new necktie, his wool sports coat.

He looked away from the mirror, and stood there. His father had not left his mind. It was not an image of his father which was with him, but a feeling, the feeling perhaps of being of the same flesh.

His father had stopped him that morning in the kitchen when they were ready to leave, and taking his shoulders in his hands, had said to him, almost politely, "I want you to remember this now. You're still young. You still have your whole life before you. You have it, and it's yours to live, no matter if they send you away for a while or not. You try to understand that. I don't know what else I can say, or what advice I can give you, except that. If they send you away—that's all right. I've thought about this. It won't matter to the size of your life. You have to understand that. It could make it bigger, if you know what I mean. Just don't let the sonsabitches get to you. You have to understand that. If you don't let them, then they can't touch you. You see what I mean? They might try to rip your guts out, for no reason at all. I've been around a few judges, and a few jailhouses, too. Well, fuck them and their automobiles. You see what I mean? You say you're sorry, and you be sorry, but don't let none of them get to you."

Alex had not quite seen what his father meant until now. It's funny, he thought—and he did not mean that it was funny at all, but that it was so strange he knew no word for it. They could not break him by sending him away. They could not do that at all, if he did not let them. He did not know what it was, only that it was there, within him now, as if in his fierce and sober words that morning his father had hammered it in to stay.

When Mr. Quinn opened the door this time, the judge did not lift his eyes from what he was reading. Alex sat down in the chair beside his father.

After a moment, again without looking up first, the judge spoke. He said, "No attempts to sell the cars or any parts thereof?"

Mr. Quinn answered. He said, "Just the one tire, sir, which was recovered."

"The brother here is three years younger?" the judge said.

"Yes, three years younger, Your Honor," Mr. Quinn said. "He was twelve at the time the cars were taken."

"On these visits, did you have your brother drive any of these cars?"

"No sir," Alex said. "I never saw him, sir."

"You never saw him?"

"I drove around. I looked for him is all, but I never saw him."

The judge made another note. When he looked up this time, he said, "Alex, please rise and step forward for sentencing."

Alex rose and stepped to within four or five feet of the desk.

Looking directly at him now, the judge said, "I'm placing you on probation until the date of your eighteenth birthday. Are you aware of the terms of probation?"

"Yes sir, I think so."

"Are you aware that I could as easily order you confined to the State Boys Vocational School at Lansing for a similar period?"

"Yes sir."

"Are you aware that if you fail to maintain the terms of this probation, you may be so confined, by order of this court, at any time during this term of probation?"

"Yes sir."

"Do you fully intend to comply with the terms of this probation?"

"Yes sir."

"Is there anything you wish to say?"

"No sir."

"Mr. Housman, please rise and stand next to your son."

His father stepped up beside him.

The judge said, "Mr. Housman, are you aware of your responsibility concerning the terms of this probation?"

"Yes, I am."

"Is there anything you wish to say?"

"No."

The judge looked down again and made another notation. Then he said, "This court is no longer in session."

Alex and his father stood in place a moment before they glanced at each other. But they did not smile; there was no feeling of victory, or of release. Then Mr. Quinn was with them, as before, directing them with a slight hand motion to follow him across the room again and into the corridor. It was like leaving a room without saying good-bye.

Down the corridor to a point beyond hearing, Mr. Quinn said softly, "That wasn't so bad, was it? He can be tough at times."

Neither of them answered. They had stopped before the elevator doors, where Mr. Quinn pressed the button. Alex stood staring at the doors, as if to concentrate on something else. The doors were unpolished, the color of lake water.

They rode down without a word. At the second floor Mr. Quinn held the elevator door a moment as he stepped out. He said, "Alex, I'll see you at about three-thirty on Thursdays, right after school. Your curfew is ten on school nights, midnight on Fridays and Saturdays—and it's nothing to take lightly."

The door closed. Alex had expected Mr. Quinn to say something in parting to his father, perhaps give him a left-handed apology for what he had said about his drinking and lack of guidance. Mr. Quinn said nothing. The man who was his father—Curly Housman—was left to deal with the charges on his own. The two of them continued down within the hum of the elevator.

Outside the courthouse they walked along the sidewalk in the sunlit cold air. Alex followed his father, in single file, for others were coming toward them, entering the building. There was a light wind, enough to swirl the vapor of Alex's breath and to cause his eyes to run at the corners.

Walking along, Alex looked at his father's back, at the sweep and fabric of his overcoat. He realized that his father overdressed; unexplainably, he realized why. The blood-colored scarf covered the back of his father's neck; high on one side, it ruffled his hair. They edged between two parked cars, walking along.

SMOKING CIGARETTES

Mickey Elliott had agreed to peddle his route on the Sunday he would be gone. But on Saturday morning, when the boy had promised to walk around with him to learn directions and customers, he was over forty minutes late. Alex sat on the curb, enjoying the warm early summer air, folding and sacking his papers, then just sitting in the early sun. He fished out a cigarette and lit it, and put it out after a puff as he realized he did not like the smell or taste of cigarettes early in the morning.

His father had still not quite agreed to drive him to the lake, but Alex believed that he would. His worry came from the vague anticipation of seeing his little brother again. They had been together always it seemed and now, for three years, they had been apart. What would Howard be like? His worry was such that when Mickey Elliott came wheeling around the corner at last, on his bicycle, Alex only smiled and said nothing at all about his being late.

Walking home, Alex kept thinking of Howard and of their mother and of the trip he was about to make. He had never questioned his father about the odd arrangement of their family, nor had his father ever offered any explanation beyond a simple comment, and Alex had not thought much about Howard's leaving until lately. Nor did it make sense even now as he walked back home. It just happened that one evening in the summer when he was twelve and Howard was nine, his father told them that Howard was going to live with their mother at the lake, where she and her new husband operated a tavern, and the next afternoon his father came home from work early, and his mother drove up after a while in her car. But when she had been in the apartment a few minutes, having a drink first with his father, and they started packing Howard's things into cardboard boxes, Alex slipped outside and down the exposed rear stairway and ran to the other side of a neighbor's garage, where he was out of sight and hearing.

He sat down there, finally, lowered into the small line of a ditch under the eave, on the washed pebbles, because he had started to cry and could not stop himself, although it helped to lean forward with his chest on his knees, to squeeze his stomach. Every time he thought it was over, and had wiped his eyes with his shirt and thought he was ready to go back, another swelling would come pushing into his throat, as if rising on the thought itself. He would strain to hold his lips together, to turn back the pressure, and would fail. His lips would be forced apart, and the sound, because he was trying to keep it low, would come out *Eeeeee-ah-Eeeeee-ah-Eeeeee* . . . with tears coming fresh from his eyes, and his heart trembling and contracting.

He did not try to understand. And it was not until he decided not to go back to the apartment that he brought himself under control. He went out along the neighbor's driveway and onto the sidewalk, and walked to a playground, where he joined a hardball game of flies-away, which he played strangely and until dark. When he went home, Howard was gone. His sports gear and jackets were gone from their hooks on the landing, and his clothes were gone from their mutual bedroom closet and from their mutual chest of drawers, and Alex had no feeling or concern over any of his own possessions or clothes being missing. He knew only that all of it hurt too much to think about. His father, drinking, made his simple comment. "Howard wasn't ours," he said.

Alex learned to forget, or not to remember. After a few days, the holes in his life that appeared throughout that first night and throughout the days that followed Howard's leaving—in the bedroom, where they had argued over a flashlight; in the bathroom, where they had argued over a certain shirt or toothpaste or over nothing he could remember; in the kitchen, where they had argued over a special pointed spoon; and in those places and at those times when they had not argued: the choosing of sides, the loaning of a glove or a dime, a playground fight when they stood together and talked about it afterwards—after a few days and some times of wondering how he could have ever cared about any of those things, these holes began to heal. Alex did not understand, and did not try to understand, even if understanding often tagged after him like the ghost of Howard himself. In the months that passed there were no visits, though the lake was less than an hour's drive from town, and all Alex knew of his brother in time was that he had changed his name to Connell. He was now Howard Connell, named after the man their mother had married.

In the apartment, Alex stood at the foot of his father's bed and squeezed one of his father's big toes, the way he always woke him. "Hey, it's really nice out—let's go," he said. It was seven-thirty by the clock on the dresser in the half-darkened bedroom.

"Okay," his father said. "Okay—go eat yourself some breakfast."

But at eight-thirty, when Alex had eaten a partial breakfast and had emptied his gym bag and repacked the bag for the trip, slipping the newly opened package of Camels into the bottom, he was still waiting, sitting at the kitchen table. He had gone to the bathroom once to offer to fix his father some eggs, but his father had told him to slow down, they had plenty of time. Alex had stood there a moment. "You're going to take a bath?" he said. "What are you taking a bath for?" And when his father came to the kitchen for the first time, barefooted and wearing clean underwear, he had nothing but a half cup of coffee, which he sipped standing up. Immediately after this, he put some ice cubes in a glass and poured himself a drink and before leaving the kitchen, said to Alex, "Stop fidgeting." Alex sat waiting.

The next time his father came to the kitchen he was wearing the pants to his powder-gray sharkskin suit, fresh from the cleaners, and his brown-and-white wingtip shoes. He was still in his ribbed and sleeveless undershirt, the dark curled hair on his chest and heavy shoulders visible, and, fixing himself another drink, he looked over at Alex and said, "You going out there looking like that?"

Alex said, "Why not?" and, as his father was leaving with another drink, added, "How about hurrying up?" but was already glancing down the front of himself and thinking, Looking like what? And in spite of looking at his dungarees and his black tennis shoes, he momentarily saw nothing and felt the same sense of possible disaster he always felt when his father was drinking.

Coming to the kitchen again, his father was still without his shirt. He fixed himself another drink. He had a bath towel tucked in around his waist to protect his pants, and he had the odor about him of having shaved. Alex sat watching him. He realized for the first time that his father was stalling, that he was acting different. Alex seldom raised the nerve to speak to his father strongly, but now it was important. "Pop, don't worry about those people," he said. "Let's get going."

His father looked at him. He paused, smiling. "Okay, let's roll!" he said. "Let's roll! What are you sitting there for?" He tipped his drink to Alex. "Get your things together," he said. He finished the drink in a long swallow, placed the glass on the table, and left the room. Alex glanced down between his feet, realizing his father was already more or less intoxicated.

In only a few minutes his father came back. He was dressed now in a fresh white shirt and a maroon silk tie, and his suit coat. He was a dresser all right. From a distance he looked like a diplomat or a banker, even though up close, as he was now, the texture of his skin and the colorations of his teeth and the watery film that covered his eyes when he drank—it covered them now—gave him away.

"Okay, partner, let's travel," he said, and Alex followed him out into the heat and down the back steps to the driveway.

His father continued to drink all the way to the lake. They said little to each other; his father fell into a mood that was not at all like his usual drinking moods. Neither drunk nor sober, he seemed at a distance. Alex sat quietly; he took a pint from under the passenger seat when it was asked for and handed it to his father. His father smacked his lips lightly and said, "*Ahhh!*" each time he drank. He kept the bottle, opened, in the crotch of his legs. Alex glanced at him once. His lips had taken on a damp color; his cheeks and neck were growing the familiar raw-plum color. Alex sat worrying, smelling the waves of whiskey. Oddly enough, for this moment, he saw why his father always bought so many pints and only occasional fifths. They were easier to hide; they fit into the glove

compartment, under the seat, into his lunch bucket. Alex glanced at his
father's profile again. Feeling afraid, he looked down the highway.

When they came to the tavern, to the sunlighted gravel parking lot,
his father pulled in and stopped in almost the same place where Alex
had stopped in a Buick Riviera he had driven here back in cold weather.
Now his father sat a full minute before he turned off the ignition. Five
or six cars were lined along the front of the tavern, facing its windows.
The dirt road beside the tavern, leading down to the houses and lakeside
cottages, was beige-colored. Finally, opening the door, his father said,
"You wait here. Let me see what's going on." He got out of the car, but
paused again. He looked through the car window with his glistening
eyes. "Son, you have to know this is pretty dumb," he said.

Alex said nothing. He glanced at his father and looked straight ahead
again.

He watched his father walk over and move between two cars opposite
the door of the tavern, passing into and out of the glare from their
hoods. The glare knifed into Alex's eyes. When he refocused, his father
was at the doorway, and he thought he saw him tip slightly to the side
as he cupped his hands to light a cigarette. Had his balance swayed from
control? Alex looked away. When he looked back again his father was
gone, the screen door was closed.

Alex looked at the channel of water where it came in beside the
tavern. It ran along beside the road, a couple of hundred feet away. He
could not see the dock, where he had stood one of those winter days, but
the dream he had carried with him all week—of visiting Howard, of
swimming and fishing, riding over the water in a boat—came to mind,
and left again, like the glare of sunlight. The smell of lake water in the
air, slightly cooler than the air from behind and smelling faintly both of
fish and pine, floated by.

Alex left the car after a moment and walked down to the dock. He
thought Howard might possibly be there, but he was not. White suds
were washing back and forth in the weeds at the edge of the water, and
he saw the silver side of a small unidentifiable fish flash in its movement. The smell was stronger here, as if the lake itself were alive. The
dream of swimming and fishing flashed through him again. It seemed
he had only to get rid of his father, that once his father was gone, the
sweeping surface of the water would present itself completely. In front

of the tavern again—the car remained empty—he looked over at the screen door and smelled the damp and stale cigarette coolness, heard the far-off lament of country music that came from within. He saw nothing beyond the sunlighted gray fabric of the screen.

He was sitting in the car when his father came out. With detachment he watched him waver just slightly into the side of one of the cars, clearly losing his balance this time. He continued, trying to appear in control of himself, a man in a handsome summer suit walking over gravel and raising powder around his brown-and-white shoes. Alex looked away.

In the car, his father sat still again. A couple of ringlets of wavy hair had fallen over one side of his forehead; he was deep red-colored now, his shirt collar looking fluorescent-white around his neck. Finally he spoke, but said only, "Your mother and Howard are down to the house. You go ahead on down. I'll be heading back."

Something had happened in the tavern. Alex had expected something to happen, had expected it all morning, still he was surprised. An image of his mother's husband came to mind, although he had yet to set eyes on the man.

"You go on now," his father said. "They're down to the house."

Alex knew he should not ask questions, but the words came out. "What about you? Aren't you going to see Howard?"

Quietly, without anger, his father said, "Son, the man doesn't want me to go down there."

Alex said nothing to this. He sat looking ahead. He remembered a morning when his father had come home with an eye so swollen that it was completely closed. A touch of the fear he had felt that morning came back to him.

His father spoke again, still softly. "It's a one-story house, white, about a half mile down—on the right-hand side." Then he said, "You want to stay?"

"We're here," Alex said, feeling immediately that he was trading this weekend, this little possible enjoyment, for something intangible and all out of proportion.

His father nodded. "You go on now," he said. "Have yourself a good time."

Alex paused. Then he took his bag in hand and opened the car door.

Outside he eased the door shut again. Bending down, he looked in through the window at his father. Their eyes met as they had few times before. His father was neither smiling nor not smiling. His eyes were pink. Softly, he said, "Slam it, son."

Alex reopened the door—the lock had not caught—and slammed it. He looked through the window again. "You coming after me tomorrow?"

"Course I'm coming after you. Go on now and enjoy yourself for a change. Catch some fish."

Alex still paused. "You—okay?" he said.

"Okay for what?"

"I don't know."

"Why'd you say that, then?"

"I don't know."

"What do you know for sure?"

"Oh, quite a bit."

They looked at each other, smiling over the humor of being father and son. His father winked. With a slight head motion he waved Alex on his way.

Alex straightened up and turned. He set off walking over the gravel toward the dirt road, listening for the car to start behind him. When he had gone a distance and the car still had not started, he wanted to look back, but knew his father would be watching him, gauging him in his intoxicated and sentimental way. Go home, Alex thought. He continued walking, his legs seeming to cover little distance. He looked back then, and although the windshield was covered with a reflection from the sun, he raised his hand and waved. He looked long enough, if his father were there, for his father to wave back.

He walked along the dirt road. Opposite a cove of water on his right, houses lined the shore. Then it was like a street in the city, with houses crowded next to one another and across the street from one another, but there were more shrubs and flowers here, many flowers in bloom, sunlighted, and the aroma of the lake water, and far off, the hum of a motor gliding through the water. At last, where the houses and road turned across the view ahead, at the turn stood a single-story white house. He realized he was trembling.

Someone was in front of the house, on the grass that ran down to the water. It was Howard, he knew it was Howard—but he could not make himself look long enough to be sure. He went on to a door at the back of the house, out of Howard's view, and paused a moment before he rapped his knuckles lightly on the glass storm door which covered a closed wooden door. He did not knock again, and waited a full minute or two. The door, the house, stood silent.

Working up his nerve at last, or perhaps losing his nerve, trembling, he walked around to the yard. There was a gate. He felt like a strange boy on the block entering the yard of a boy who had always lived there. His vision felt awry, as if he were glancing away from something without moving his head.

"Hey—hullo," he said, his voice off-key.

Howard was doing something over a wooden box. Looking up, he did not speak.

"What're you doing there?" Alex said.

"Well look who's here," Howard said.

Alex was vaguely shocked by Howard's appearance—the change and growth that had taken place. Still, his face, and a vein of his voice, were recognizable, as though his features had remained nearly constant while his face had grown longer and thinner, his voice deeper. "It's me," Alex said, and walking over, he seemed to look away, at the ground, to the side, his face asserting its own foolish control.

"I wasn't sure at first," Howard said. "You sure have changed a lot."

"So have you."

"Boy, does your voice sound different," Howard said.

"You should hear yours."

"Gee, I didn't think anyone could get uglier but you managed all right for yourself," Howard said. He finished his line weakly, laughing uncertainly, as if he had been rehearsing its delivery all week. Alex joined him laughing, smiling.

"What's that stuff?" Alex said. "What are you doing?" He indicated the box, a handful of dirt Howard held in his hand.

Howard let the dirt, along with several night crawlers, fall back into the box. "My worm box," he said. "I been gathering some worms, in case we want to go fishing. I got over three hundred." He replaced a cover on the box, and then nearly whispered, "Listen, we should get

away from here in a hurry or I'll have to clean the garage or something."
He began moving toward a small white dock and a boat tied there, and
Alex placed his bag beside the worm box and followed. "Where's Pop?"
Howard said. "In the house?"

"He already went back," Alex said, nodding over his shoulder, feeling a slight heart shiver. He thought about saying something of his
father being sorry not to see Howard, and expected Howard to say
something, but neither of them spoke.

On the dock they were awkwardly silent with each other, looking at
the boat and the outboard motor afloat beside them, getting in each
other's way once. "You can run this thing?" Alex said. Howard nodded,
and lifting a rope over a post, gripped the boat and presented it for Alex
to climb in. Alex stepped in and the boat gave on the water and he
almost lost his balance. Howard laughed, as did Alex, sitting down.
"Where's—Mother?" Alex asked, nodding toward the house.

Howard did not say. He was crouching on the dock, hand-sliding the
boat along in the water.

"Shouldn't we go see her?"

"Nah, we'll see her later." Howard pushed the boat away from the
dock, drawing himself in beside the motor.

Alex had a feeling that something important had been left unsettled,
but he sat on the wooden seat, watching Howard work with the motor,
and said nothing. Within a moment, on the third pull of the rope, the
motor's sputtering caught, and Howard turned and looked past Alex to
the open water.

Howard looked ahead, over Alex's shoulder, and Alex looked at him
directly for a moment. He seemed no larger than the motor he now
controlled. He was twelve. In a moment he turned his eyes to Alex and
smiled, proud of himself, of his lake, of running the boat. Alex smiled
back. Looking away again—over the motor's roar there was nothing to
say—he shifted more around to look ahead. With the warm sun coating
his back, he looked ahead, over the open water, feeling the spray and
seeing an endless distance within, seeing his father.

Without warning, Howard turned the handle to full power. The
motor roared with the noise of an airplane, the front of the boat leaping,
slapping the water once like an opened hand, as Alex, thrust back,
grabbed the sides with both hands in order not to tumble backward.

Alex turned to see a wind-whipped smile on Howard's face. They left a deep churning V behind them now, the water spraying, spattering up from both sides. In the roar and acceleration—they were skimming, bouncing over the surface of green water—something of the promise of the week came home to Alex.

They swept out into the lake in a circle, banged over their own waves. They stopped once and bobbed in their wake. Later Howard shouted over the motor that they had to get gas, and crossing the long mouth of a cove, they entered a channel. Howard still drove the boat forcefully through the water, leaving boats tied along docks on the two sides bobbing. Alex held the sides of the boat. In a few minutes, down the channel, he saw the back of the tavern coming into view. LAKESIDE TAVERN was painted in black on salmon stucco. He knew it was possible his father was still there, waiting around. His father had done those things—had come around the ball fields when he was supposed to be at work. Once, playing baseball, Alex had noticed from his position that his father was over on the street, sitting in the car, but when Alex slipped over between innings to see him, his father told him it was nothing, told him to go back to his ball game, and drove off a minute later.

Alex glanced around at the bank and at what he could see of the parking lot as they approached, but he saw no one. Howard cut the motor, the boat sank its belly into the water, and they sputtered up and stopped, as the motor stopped, beside the red gas pump. Howard, tying the boat's rope around a post, said they had to get the key, and started up the bank toward the rear of the tavern. Alex lagged back, until Howard turned and said, "Come on."

Howard held the back door open. They passed through a small dark room filled with beer cases and folded tables, and opening another door, came into the cool tavern behind one end of the bar. The man down the bar had to be Ward Connell. He stood opposite three or four men. Alex had imagined him to be small, or wiry, or homely—a stubby sailor—but he was taller than his father and younger-looking. He wore a short-sleeved sport shirt and looked very sober. He said "Hi" to Howard, and glanced past Howard to Alex.

Alex stayed back in the doorway and waited as Howard and Ward talked to each other. He imagined his father entering the bar in his powder-gray suit and brown-and-white shoes. He wondered how they had talked to each other. Had they talked right there with those other men listening and watching? The images which came to mind were not pleasant, as if that hard stomach of his father's and his bricklike arms were strong only for him, as if here in this dark building, they had not counted for much at all.

He noticed Howard and Ward both looking at him as Howard was talking, and he noticed also that some of the men along the bar were looking his way. He thought they must know he was the son of the man Ward had talked to ("Ward, listen, I got my boy out here in the car . . ."). He thought they looked too long not to know something. He made no move, but all his fear and shyness sharpened to a needle point and left him, and he looked directly back at them.

Howard made no introductions. Leaving Ward then, he came back to Alex with a ring of keys. Ward called out behind them, "You guys want some pop, help yourself."

Alex decided he would have no pop. If his father had been behind that bar, he thought, he would have come over to shake hands and make him feel welcome. His father *was* a kind and generous man, he thought. In the small room, where Howard was lifting the iron handle of a wooden cooler door—laughter came from back in the bar and a knife rose in Alex's chest as the laughter rose—Alex said, "No, I don't want any."

Howard ignored him and pulled out two bottles. "Sure you do," he said.

Down on the dock Howard handed Alex one of the bottles, which he took, Nehi strawberry, as Howard worked a jackknife from his pocket. Alex hesitated, and wishing at once, even as he was doing it, that he had not, he heaved the bottle perhaps fifty feet out into the channel. The bottle hit in a splash and disappeared. Beside him, Howard said kindly, "What's the matter?"

"Nothing."

"What did you do that for?"

"I just didn't want it."

"Why are you so mad?"

"I'm not. Forget it."

After a pause, Howard said, "We can play shuffleboard later. If it's not crowded."

"How about going fishing?"

"It's too late now," Howard said. "Wait'll later. Fish never bite this time of day."

Howard, his bottle of pop placed on the dock, unlocked the pump and knelt to pump gas into a red can on the floor of the boat. He looked up, and he and Alex looked at each other for a moment, and then he looked back to the pumping.

Alex sat in the boat as Howard ran back to return the key. Howard was gone so long that Alex imagined them whispering about him. He thought of his father again. He imagined him driving back to the city, on the highway, alone. He imagined him back in the apartment, alone. He had never felt his father's loneliness as he did now. He was relieved now that his mother was not in the tavern when they first arrived.

They knew no words for apology, and Howard, returning, offered the driving of the boat to Alex, which Alex accepted. He guided the boat back along the channel toward the open water of the lake. He had thought all week of a moment like this, driving ahead as if he were only going from one place to another. Howard, looking over his shoulder, said, "Hey, give it some gas."

Alex turned the handle. The motor roared; the front of the boat rose, pointing up. But nothing beyond the noise and slamming movement of the boat seemed to be happening. Alex felt little excitement. Howard was shouting; he motioned down with his hand.

Alex did not slow the motor. He held the handle tight and looked ahead, around the side of the boat, as if he had not understood Howard's signal. Howard stopped waving and held on, partially standing, looking ahead himself. The boats along the channel rose and fell in their wake.

Entering the open water, going a distance, Alex's feelings of rage sank away. He turned the handle and abruptly the boat settled into the water. Howard looked back at him. Alex smiled, and Howard smiled in return. The motor stopped; they bobbed quietly in a vacuum of sound.

"I forgot how crazy you can be," Howard said.

Alex laughed a little. "You better drive this thing," he said.

*   *   *

In the afternoon, back at the house, Alex met his mother. She smiled at him. Her deep voice surprised his memory with recognition. "What happened to your dad?" she asked him.

"He had to get back," Alex said.

His mother was wearing a silk housecoat and drinking coffee standing up. She said nothing more of his father. She looked him over and said he was certainly growing up. She asked him how he had been getting along, how school was—he was in the eleventh grade now, wasn't he? He gave short answers—he was fine, he'd be in eleventh grade in the fall—wondering if she was going to ask about the cars, the detention home, his hearing and probation. Going to her bedroom to dress, she called back to Howard to fix him and Alex some lunch. Howard called back that they had already eaten, and he nodded to Alex and they slipped out quietly and escaped in the boat, back to the tavern, to play shuffleboard.

There were more people in the tavern now, including a couple of women. Music was playing on the jukebox. This time Ward said, "Hi, there," and Alex said, "Hi."

The tavern was cool, a dark place lighted at midday. Everyone seemed to know everyone else. They seemed happy with the day, or with the summertime. Howard taught Alex how to play shuffleboard and Alex tried to pay attention. But as they played he felt that Ward was keeping an eye on him. He did not think why, only that he felt out of place. When a group at the bar laughed he wondered if they were laughing about his father, if the men who had been there earlier were now telling to the women the story of what Ward had said to this guy in his fancy suit and two-tone shoes.

Glimpsing his life back in the city, Alex saw a world which was quiet and lonely. He also saw that his father, back in the city, would be in trouble and dangerous today, and it seemed this was the first time he had ever understood why.

He did not recognize his mother when she first came in the front door of the tavern. Then the recognition was overwhelming; she looked as she had the several times she came to visit. She wore a shining summer dress, or a springtime dress, a ruffle of something white outlining a deep V down her throat, and makeup, lipstick, faint powder, high-heeled shoes. People along the bar turned on their stools and called to her, called her Maggie and looked happy if she spoke to them, happy to see her. Alex felt a remote pride that she was his mother, that she was so attractive. She talked to several people along the bar, laughing and throwing her head back, stopping several minutes with some and a moment with others, until she was at the end of the bar and ducked under to come up on the other side. Another man was working with Ward, an older man—Alex had not noticed him before—and Alex heard him say to her, "How's my sweetheart?"

Alex looked at her occasionally from the shuffleboard. He wanted to look at her and was afraid he would be seen. After a while she came over. She told Howard this would have to be their last game—it was getting too crowded. She looked at Alex and smiled warmly, and asked if he was enjoying himself. There was a scent of flowers about her, and a slight rustling of her silk dress around her legs. He nodded, he even smiled; music from the jukebox allowed him not to speak.

She leaned close, however, and she said, "Honey, I just wanted to say to you, if you smoke, that you don't encourage Howard. Okay? It's none of my business if you do, I just don't want Howard to get started. Will you do that for me?"

"Yes," he said. "Sure."

In the evening, when the sun was down and the boats had left the lake, after a meal of potato chips and root beer in the empty house, they went fishing. Alex asked Howard if he ate every night like this and Howard nodded with an embarrassed smile that he did. Alex himself was in a melancholy mood in the quiet house. He asked Howard if he ever tried to fix himself a meal. Howard said, "Sometimes," and Alex thought it was a lie.

Howard was not allowed to take the boat on the water after sundown and they fished from the bank, using night crawlers from the wooden box. Facing the house for light from the windows, Howard showed him how to hook two of the long worms onto the hook so they made a gob, and tentatively at first, Alex reached into the dirt in the wooden box.

They caught dozens of bullheads. They fished just off the bank in the shallow water, catching most of the bullheads before they knew they were hooked, throwing them back on the grass at once, on Howard's instructions, shaking them loose—or, in the air, surrendering their ferocious appetites, the bullheads let go on their own—and flopped around the grass in the dark until they made it back through the frog-hair into the water. Some they unhooked by holding them underfoot, avoiding their horns, using pliers to take the hook from their small grinding teeth and throats—some of the bullheads squeaked faintly—catching still others almost at once on the same gob of worms.

The air grew completely dark, but they could still see the red-and-white bobbers on their lines reflecting the house lights behind them. Alex enjoyed himself now for more than a few minutes at a time. He was without any fear. When he felt the line go taut, felt it pull and tremble, bending the rod, zigzagging and cutting water as the fish took the bobber down into the blackness and out of sight, there was nothing else to think about.

The night air remained warm. Fish thumped now and then behind them on the grass, and the frogs and insects around the edge of the water were singing, buzzing, croaking in a continuous hum, as if to fill the air, to deny any space for thinking. Lights from other houses and cottages ran over the water, along with occasional voices or music or laughter. Near midnight they kicked the fish back into the water, kicked them because Howard said they would stick their fingers with their horns if they picked them up. Howard said the bullheads were tough fish and could do something special with their gills to stay alive for hours out of water, but they did not count or watch to see if any of the fish failed to swim down and away into the darkness.

Alex was pleasantly tired. Before going to sleep, lying on a cot in the small bedroom off the kitchen he shared with Howard, he had the thought that he had gone on to start a new part of his life. He had a vision for a moment of himself being above his father's confusion, of having passed through it as a stranger. Howard lay in his own bed opposite, in the dark room. They talked some, softly, of school, of teachers, taking turns telling things. Howard asked him no questions about their father and his drinking. Nor did he ask about the cars, or the detention home. Alex would not have minded, as if he had turned a corner on those times as well.

*   *   *

Voices woke him during the night. They raised him from full sleep to half-waking. He recognized after a moment the strange bed with its damp smell, and remembered where he was, realized they were not the voices of his father and some woman he had brought home. There was a line of dull white along the bottom of the bedroom door, and the voices were close by, from the kitchen.

There were four or five of them. Laughter was around everything they said. Alex looked across the room toward Howard's bed, but heard nothing, could see nothing of him in the darkness. He had an idea they were both lying there awake, listening, thinking, both of them somehow caught this way. He considered whispering to Howard, considered talking to him to somehow straighten out in their own way this confusion that had them listening in the dark, and afraid. But Alex was not sure of the idea, not sure of Howard, nor of himself, and he could not bring himself to speak.

There were both men and women in the kitchen. Alex knew Ward's voice, although he had only heard it once or twice, but his mother's voice sounded different. He listened to her tell how she and Em Lewis had decided to open a lakeside whorehouse with the dock out there lined with red lights. They all laughed as she talked. (Was Em Lewis a man or a woman?) Every time she used the word "whore," although his father used language much stronger than that, Alex felt a slight shock. He lay still and listened, or did not try not to listen, until the people left. He listened then to Ward and his mother talking farther away in the house, talking more casually and without much laughter, and he listened for a time thereafter to the wandering of his mind.

Waking at daylight, he recognized again the sheets and the room. The voices from the night, as well as Howard's and his own when they were catching bullheads, were like voices in dreams and difficult to play over in daylight. Birds were singing outside now, and far over the lake, after a moment, he heard a lone motor approach and pass, moving beyond hearing. According to the way he guessed the time in the morning at home, by the sun and the feel of the air, he thought it must be no more than five or five-thirty. He worried about his paper route. Mickey Elliott would not be up yet, would not finish before ten or eleven o'clock, would probably miss a dozen houses.

He rose quietly from the cot, in his undershorts and T-shirt, and stood there. He looked over at Howard. Howard lay with his eyes closed, holding his pillow. His upper lip and nose were curved up against the pillow, and his T-shirt was yellowish-looking against the gray, wilted sheets. He was asleep. Alex could see and hear the rising and falling of his breath. Howard was underweight; his arms, out over his head, were too small. Alex had no thought of talking to him, waking him, not in the daylight, which held none of the intimacy the night had held. Alex looked at him, and for a moment he was unable to look away. Howard Connell.

In the kitchen Alex crossed the linoleum floor on his bare toes and looked through the glass panel of the kitchen door. The dirt road that ran back to the tavern was empty, its surface lightly coated with dew. He thought of the full day to go. Waiting for his father. Would he come to the house? What would he and Ward say to each other now?

On his way to the bathroom, he saw something that made his heart actually jump. They were naked. Their bedroom door was open and they lay asleep, in a tangle, naked. He went on to the bathroom, but once he was there he was unable to urinate. Standing back, leaning against the cool tile wall, he let out a deep breath.

After a moment he went back, eight or ten steps through the quiet house. He looked in their bedroom door. They had not moved. He stared at the woman who happened to be his mother. He looked at her as if she were a girl or a teacher at school and Ward's body was not there. He looked at her breasts, which were large and full-looking where they lay upon her ribs. The nipples were black-purple and darker than her hair, almost the color of her lipstick. He wanted to keep looking, but he imagined them opening their eyes now and catching him. He walked over, into the kitchen, and stood for a moment. The linoleum was cool on his bare feet. He thought he could hear their breathing behind him. He could hear his own.

Passing their door again, he glanced in and saw that they had moved. They continued to sleep, but their bodies had shifted. His mother was entirely visible now, even the patch of hair between her legs. He paused long enough in passing to look her over again, to look at the powdery and deep smoothness of her flesh against the darker hairy background of Ward. Going on, thoughts were moving in his mind with the wavering quality of weeds seen deep in the green water from the boat. He thought of his father. He thought of Ward telling his father not to go to the house. He thought also of Howard and of his mother, not knowing what it was he was thinking. For a moment then, the things in his life that had been confusing seemed to be rising from the confusion, seemed to be focusing into clarity. But the moment blurred quickly.

In the bedroom, Howard was still sleeping. Alex looked at him again. And he nearly looked away, nearly turned to climb back into bed to let the day carry him along and work itself out. Then the knowledge came to him. After all this time. Howard was not his brother.

He left the bedroom again. He passed the door on his way to the bathroom and glanced in to see them sleeping as before. When he had finished in the bathroom, he paused a moment, trying to decide whether or not to flush the toilet in the Sunday-morning stillness. Then he flushed it. He held the handle down as if to prolong its gushing-sucking roar, as if to announce what he knew to them all. He thought of his father, and closed his eyes for a moment.

When he came from the bathroom, their door was closing its last several inches. They had to know he had seen them.

Howard continued to sleep. Alex's gym bag was there by the foot of the cot he had slept in, but when he had picked it up and decided to leave, he almost grew confused again. Then things seemed clear again. If they stopped him now, if he had to wait the full day for his father, the day looked as long as the entire summer. He decided they would not stop him, he would not allow them to stop him. He would run if he had to, or fight; they would see.

When he had dressed, had packed his things into his bag and quietly drawn the zipper, and at last looked over, he saw that Howard was watching him. Howard lay with his eyes open, looking frightened.

Howard said, without condemnation, "Where you going?"

Alex paused, looking at him. "Home," he said.

"What's the matter?" Howard said.

"Nothing," Alex said.

"Why do you have to go home?" Howard said.

"I don't know," Alex said. "I just feel like it."

"Don't you want to go fishing some more?"

Alex hesitated, looking down. Looking over at Howard, he said, "No. Not now."

They looked at each other for a moment, both of them trying, it seemed, to hold on and not lose control.

Alex spoke again; his voice was clear, although high. "You know what I'm going to do," he said. "I haven't told anyone. I'm going to join the army."

"What about school?"

"I lost it at school."

Howard looked at him, offered no other response.

"I'll write to you from the army," Alex said. "That's what I meant."

Howard's eyes were glossing over, and Alex did not know what else to say. As he knew he was starting to break, he said, "Listen, I'll see you sometime. Just go back to sleep."

He opened the bedroom door, looking away from Howard, and stepped out. He closed the door behind him, carefully and not completely. Stepping to the kitchen door, he began feeling confused again, thinking he should stay, he should go back. He seemed to see a deeper loneliness in Howard's life, in spite of his motorboat and his lake, than in his own. He wished he had gotten around to telling him not to smoke.

The air helped. It was warmer without than within. He carried his bag along the carpet-soft dirt road. The dew from the night had left a velvet texture over the powder of dirt and he concentrated on breaking the texture with his footprints. In a moment, some distance away, he heard a truck's tires sing as it passed on the highway. He walked along. He tried to make his mind think of something, of anything, and thought of the city, imagined his papers lying on the curb untouched. He thought of his father. He imagined being there in the city, and remembered how quiet and hot it was on Sunday afternoons. He imagined his father asleep in his bedroom, with the fan on his dresser sweeping back and forth so slowly. He'd probably be asleep in his shirt and tie and suit pants.

He passed the tavern. The gravel parking lot was empty of cars and stale-looking with litter. He thought of Ward, without thinking of anything much in particular, and turned then to walk along on the shoulder of the highway.

Maybe this afternoon he would go to a movie. Yes, he would. He wished he were there now, as he sensed the feeling of hiding in the cool darkness and giving himself to the world on the screen. In the afternoon the Coney Island would have its windows opened to the sidewalk, the grill just inside the window lined with rows of pink glistening hot dogs, the baseball game from Detroit coming over a radio. He felt homesick for the city, even for its tedium on a Sunday.

At a crossroads, at an old country Sunoco station, he tried to call home. Standing at a wall phone, his bag between his feet, he felt inhibited by a man sitting behind a greasy, littered desk. There was no answer. He let the phone ring, far off on the kitchen counter, seven, eight, nine times, intending each time to hang up and letting it ring once more.

Back across the highway, he walked again, listening for cars to come along. He removed his cigarettes and matches from his bag and lit up. He walked on, smoking. He listened for cars and each time one approached he stepped onto the soft shoulder to lay out his thumb and walk backwards with the sun in his face.

ABOUT THE AUTHOR

Theodore Weesner grew up in Flint, Michigan. He left school at sixteen, spent three years in the army, and later attended Michigan State University and the University of Iowa. His first novel, *The Car Thief*, won the Great Lakes Writers Prize, and a later novel, *The True Detective*, was cited by the American Library Association as one of the notable books of 1987. His short fiction has appeared in *The New Yorker*, *Esquire*, *The Atlantic Monthly*, *Ploughshares*, and *Best American Short Stories*. He lives in Portsmouth, New Hampshire, and teaches at Emerson College in Boston.